Steele Shield

Kimberly Amato

Little Crown Media, LLC

For Michelle (The Mighty McT) who reminds me daily what true integrity and strength mean.
For my niece Hope, who fills my days with laughter, love, and Mickey balloons.
Fly high, little one.

Contents

Forward

I *don't want to die.*

These words pour out of the victim like a mantra. Like a prayer thrown up to the heavens, each syllable heard by those who choose torturous means as a way of life, a freelancer of fear in a world of the mundane. It's the climax of the longer feature that they've written, directed, and produced . . . starring you. Only you are unaware of your casting.

The first act is always the same in its humble, creative beginnings. An "accidental" meeting in the coffee shop where you get your morning beverage every day. A smile as you get on the 1 subway train uptown to work. You're never quite sure where they come from or leave to, yet those fleeting moments bolster a fictitious relationship.

The second act is the meat and bones of the performance. The flirting is obvious to individuals nearby but oblivious to you. Your polite replies, nonsensical conversation, and compassion were never meant as anything more. Yet, they look between the lines and form a connection that you have inadvertently laid out like a lighthouse in the darkness. They're drawn to you, word by word, scene by scene. They pull closer to you daily, saving you a seat on the crowded subway or ordering your coffee ahead of time exactly how you like it. Everything is a scripted maneuver to make the string of fate between you two stronger. Every smile you give in return is an invitation to everything that you are.

Toward the end of act two, things begin to raise red flags of concern for you, the soon-to-be victim. You begin to pull away, avoid the situation at all costs, and politely decline every request. The normal response would be to walk away, but they will pester you for another chance, a moment to explain. Eventually, the ties of fate will be severed on your side and the memory of those moments will fade into the obscurity of time.

If you're lucky, they'll skip the next part and jump to the end via social media. They'll call you out as a cocktease, a whore, a mentally ill person, or various other unsavory names to denigrate your person. Maybe their feed will encompass long-threaded diatribes of vitriol at your lack of interest. They will twist every encounter to ensure they're never seen as the guilty party or show any signs of impropriety, all the missives carefully constructed to fit their narrative and subsequent film. These actions will hurt, but their fifteen minutes of fame will be pushed down the scroll of news when another scandal breaks. You'll lower your defenses and life will move on, but this will always be attached to your name on a Google search. It will make you permanently suspicious of those who come into your life.

But you're not lucky. And they're not gone.

In act three, nothing you see is true, and they feel everything is permitted. The same train rides that you once looked forward to are now mired in that subtle feeling of someone watching. Out of view, steps behind—watching you from a safe distance—they continue their quest. They create detailed records of your weekly routines, a psychopath stalking their prey. The hairs stand up on the back of your neck at the odd notion of something amiss, but there's no evidence to support it. Coming home to your haven, you swear the laundry hadn't been folded this morning and the dishes washed. Yet, these completed actions don't fully put you on alert.

After a suitable amount of time with no appreciation or response from you, they push the project to its crescendo. The orchestra strings kick into action as you unlock your front door. The trumpets sound as your shoe crunches on the ceramic plates smashed on your floor, the Bambi lamp your mother gave you as a child in pieces under your heels. The drums pound as you walk farther into your home. Clothing slashed. Photos shredded and frames broken. The flutes creep in as you realize only your truly prized possessions were destroyed. You know now how serious those fleeting moments were, the pieces almost audibly clicking one by one into the larger picture.

The *pièce de resistance*: a printed photo of you and your boyfriend laying discarded in the bathroom. You remember the trip downtown and the romantic walk in the park, but not the zoomed-in shot of your smiling faces. The words *vos es meus* are written in your scarlet red lipstick above it, your significant other's face painted over with the same color. The fear crawls up your spine. Your hand scratches your skin, trying to quell the feeling of roaches creeping over every inch of you. Your brain shuts down, and on autopilot, you go to the only place you know is safe . . .

. . . to chosen family.

Chapter One

The sun rose a few hours ago, and my best friend Hadley finally fell asleep around the same time. She came over in the early morning hours when most people are sleeping or heading home from the bars, her voice shaky, hands trembling as the description of her ruined apartment flowed out of her. As she spoke, the full image of the physical and emotional damage were constructed in my mind, the stalking laws running through my mind's eye, one row at a time. As her tears slowly subsided, the realization that this would be the hardest case we will ever face caused goose bumps. Not because she's family or the possible difficulty in gathering evidence given the intrusion of her home. My heart aches with slight fear because these types of cases are difficult to prove. The laws are so gray and lax enough that a person can walk through them. If paparazzi can easily follow you anywhere with freedom of speech as their badge of protection, it's relatively easy for anyone else to do the same—restraining order or not.

Since I heard Hadley's first snores, I've been sitting in the kitchen trying to get my bearings with all of the changes in the last twenty-four hours: The case against a prominent military man for killing a serial killer. His actions, which removed the chance for us to find his last victim alive, are still reflected in all the major headlines. That insanity gave way to my wedding—an emotional turn going from that conflicting case to standing up with my fiancée Frankie and committing ourselves to forever. Years of ups and downs, loss, and job schedule differences finally culminated in the most beautifully simple ceremony.

The weight of the black tungsten wedding ring feels foreign on my finger—a reminder of our relationship, but also of the responsibility it represents. Frankie, the go-to psychologist for the police department, is worthy of everything this world can offer, and it's my job to give her the attention that our marriage deserves. My mother always told me marriage was a job riddled with arguments, compromises, and wonderful moments. You can either enjoy the ride, or you can shirk your duties and watch the entire thing crumble. I want the ride—the whole damn, dirty thing.

"If you wanted to play videogames on our wedding night, all you had to do was ask," Frankie says, walking into the kitchen, wiping the sleep from her eyes as her nostrils flare at the scent of freshly brewed coffee. "You made coffee?"

"Just a few minutes ago. I know your alarm goes off at six." The lemon ginger tea slides down my throat, trying to wake me up with its warmth. Thanks to several doctors, my nephew, and Frankie, my overwhelming caffeine addiction was kicked to the curb. "I didn't *want* to play games . . ." The words slide out, beginning the defense of my evening's actions.

"It's okay, my love. I finally read up on *Mass Effect*. Supposedly, that blue chick is really hot. I'm sure that's why you're playing it." The low rumble from her chest betrays her attempt to tease me. She pours herself a cup of black coffee and turns her attention back to me. Her matching wedding band shines in the kitchen light.

"First off, her name is Liara. Secondly, she's an Asari, not just a blue chick. Thirdly, I was only playing so I could stay awake for Captain Zeile's call."

Hadley's sleepy grunts mixed with fearful moans waft into the kitchen. Frankie walks to the entryway to the living room, peeks inside, and squints to see the shadowy figure in the dark. Without saying a word, she sits across the table from me and proceeds to take a sip of her coffee.

"Want to explain why our friend who has enough money to rent a place in Manhattan is crashing on our couch?"

The words swirl in my mind, making it impossible to explain clearly what Hadley is going through. Not knowing the specific details that were lost behind sobs and snot or an update from Zeile makes me even more hesitant to bastardize it when sharing.

"Jasmine, why is my best friend sleeping on our couch hugging your old teddy bear?" She gives me a look that screams "answer me or sleep on the floor since the couch is taken." The false strength hides the fear that creeps into her eyes before rolling down her arms and into her fingers, which tense around her mug.

"I'm waiting on clarification, so I'm going to say this clinically," I answer. "Hadley came over here, upset and shaking. She had gone home after filming, and her place was broken into. She mentioned things being destroyed, but I couldn't make out what clearly. So, I called the captain, and he went over there with a team. I've been waiting on his call ever since." My eerily calm tone sends an unexpected shiver through my body. Maybe it's how formulaic everything sounds, or just pure exhaustion. I don't have time to figure out which.

"Doesn't she live in a building with a doorman and security? How'd they manage to get in?" Frankie asks.

"She took several photos of the scene. She assumed they came through the window."

"There are bars on the damn things. How the hell can someone get in without anyone noticing?"

"Yes, they do have bars. Hadley said they were cut," I begin. "Again, this is all based on the photos, but it's a rational theory with the fire escape there. That's all I have, Frankie. I can't give you any answers when I don't have them."

"I'm not asking you to," she says. Her voice escalates to a somewhat threatening level before she takes a deep breath and exhales it slowly. "I just . . . I don't know if I can handle this again."

"I know, honey." I reach across the table and rest my hand on top of hers.

"Do you? Really understand, I mean?"

"She's our best friend, our family . . . I was there when Garrison kidnapped her because of his father's obsession. I remember how she looked caged up. It's crystal clear when I think about it, but the case is closed. Garrison is dead, his father behind bars for life. I understand more than you know."

"Yes, all of that, but you forget the rest. You never mention how my wife was convinced to go alone and play the hero while I slept in the room next to our son. You don't know how that felt, Jasmine. I don't think you'll ever know the hopelessness that filled me. You're smarter than that, and yet you did it anyway."

"In my defense, I thought her protection was there as my backup. I had no reason to believe there was an accomplice."

"That may be true, but it isn't the point." Frankie pauses, and I force myself to shut my mouth and wait for her to finish talking. "When anyone in your chosen or biological family is in trouble, you run headfirst into the abyss to save them. You promised me you wouldn't do that anymore. You can't just send us all away until you figure out what's going on here!" Frankie's anxiety pumps out of her body like bass on the dance floor. I wait several seconds for her to calm her breathing before I begin to speak.

"I know I've put myself in harm's way, but life is very different now." The words come out like a soothing poem rather than heavy metal music. "I have a team around me I trust with my life. I have a kid I'm responsible for, and Frankie . . . I finally have you. I don't have a death wish or a desire to run off into the afterlife. I've built something here, and I'd like to enjoy it for as long as possible before someone tries to eradicate it right before my eyes, okay?"

Chase, our nephew by law but our son by practice, walks into the room. His pajamas are smaller than his frame, pant legs rising above his ankles, sleeves ending at the forearm, and a sliver of his stomach hanging out. We tried to donate them a few months ago, but he refused to come out of his room for the rest of his life if we did. Frankie told me to pick my battles; we'll make them disappear when we replace them with a bigger size. "Why are you guys fighting?" The grogginess in his voice reminds me of his father's voice in the mornings. Frankie is out of her chair and pulling him into a hug before I can form any response in my head.

"No, sweetie, we're not fighting," Frankie says.

"You just got married. You can't break up again. I don't want that." The seriousness in his pout and his arms tightly wrapped around my wife's neck back up his refusal to let either one of us go.

"I know, love, but we're just talking a little louder than we should have been. I promise." She kisses him on the forehead. "Now, why don't you go upstairs and get ready for school, okay? I'll make you breakfast."

"Fruit Loops?" he asks with the same puppy dog eyes she gets from me.

Frankie caves. "Yes, fine, but just for today."

Chase rushes up the stairs like a stampede of bison across the plains. Thankfully, when Hadley conks out, she could sleep through a nuclear war, so the noise won't wake her.

"Promise me," she says.

"Already did that and got the shirt to prove it."

"I'm serious, Jasmine. Promise me you won't run into the unknown without proper backup."

The feet of the chair screech across the floor as I stand, pulling my wife into a tight hug. I breathe in the scent of her hair as her hands press firmly on my back.

"I give you my word that I'll be as careful as possible, considering my job. If you or Chase are in danger though . . . all bets are off. That's all I can do."

"I'll make peace with that." She kisses my neck before leaning back in the embrace. "I knew who you were when we started dating and when we got married. I worry about you every moment you're out there."

"Trust the team and me."

"It's not you or them I don't trust. It's everyone else." She steps closer to me. "Have you spoken to Karina since the news broke?"

"No, she's not answering my calls. Other than Simon's conviction, I don't know what to believe. You know how it is."

"I do. Just let her know we're here for her. Simon's crimes are his and his alone. She isn't responsible for his choices."

"True, but guilt doesn't care. It just overwhelms your emotions."

"I know, but it doesn't negate the truth." She kisses my neck once before walking away and up the stairs. Lack of sleep weighs me down, and my body slumps back into the chair nearest to me. My head falls onto my arms as my eyes beg to close in relief. Every fiber of my being begs for respite from the mostly all-nighter. The days of staying awake forty-eight hours to study or to dance at clubs long expired with my youth.

The vibration of my cell phone signals the end to my fantasy of sleep. Reaching across the table, I flip the phone up to read the caller ID. It's Zeile.

"Hey, Cap." My low, gravelly voice sounds foreign to my ears, as if I've smoked a million cigarettes over my lifetime.

"We've been through Ms. Moreno's place thoroughly. Will's on the way to pick you up and bring you here. Sydney will stay at your place in the meantime."

"Cap, everything okay? I appreciate the extra security, but should we move Hadley somewhere off the grid?"

"Not at the moment. Right now, I need to know if Ms. Moreno remembers seeing anything missing or out of place when she came in."

"Understood." I clear my throat. "She took some pictures, so we can compare them to the tech's images. Maybe they came back."

"Just get here." His authoritative voice ends the call.

***

The doorman and the security officer stand to the left of the lobby entrance. Police officers frantically write down whatever the two men are saying. I'm sure they're giving an overabundance of information given the high-profile clients that live here. If any of the homeowners lose confidence in the person behind the desk, they're fired. The landlord can't afford a bad reputation. I wonder if they've been in touch already, asking for the lights to be turned off outside or the police presence to be isolated to Hadley's floor.

The elevator ride to the sixth floor is slow. The music that fills the small box is from my childhood, a small reminder of how I've aged over the years. The elevator panel is missing the number thirteen, as per tradition or superstition. The small button camera in the corner records everything discretely. Mirrors surround you, leaving nothing to the imagination but also making the space feel larger.

The elevator smoothly stops on Hadley's floor. The doors open to bedlam. People mill about everywhere. Crime scene investigators are scouring every inch of the small hallway as they speak to one another about what was already covered. Once I step out onto the designer tile, the sounds stop. Each individual turns their attention toward me, and the discomfort settles in my stomach. I wonder if they're concerned that I'll snap like I almost did when my brother died. Maybe they're worried I'm too close to the case. Either way, I understand their fear is warranted. I am too close, and I have lost my cool. But I'm here.

I remember how happy Hadley was when she found this place. It's a small building, only five floors, with a classic feel, and completely renovated. The small, gated courtyard is a rarity in the city. The East Side location was perfect for her; she felt safe and still connected to her life before money came into the picture. The place wasn't cheap, but it felt safe. At least it used to.

The only door at the end of the hallway, number five, is open and covered in various patches of black powder. Fingerprints were lifted long before I arrived. A locksmith is on his knees, working diligently to replace the old bolts with new ones. The landlord must have sent him. I'm surprised Zeile permitted him to contaminate the crime scene.

The grayish-blue paint of the hallway suffered the same fate at the door— blotched with black powder and other chemicals. Techs kneel on the floor searching every inch for any residue of any kind. I'll be honest, I've not seen this kind of response to a scene. I wonder if it's due to the high-profile nature of the case or the new team. I hope it's the latter since the former would leave me angry for those not related to a cop or at Hadley's level.

The floor in the main entryway to her condo is littered with a small amount of broken glass or porcelain; I can't quite tell which. They must have collected it as evidence before I got here, but some pieces remain. The large, open living space has floor-to-ceiling windows on the outer wall, a nice-sized kitchen on the opposite one, and a small breakfast bar separating the two sections. Plainclothes and uniformed officers fill both areas, making it feel claustrophobic.

The LED television is on, but it's broken; the line of black from the left moves across like a sine wave to the other side of the screen. The top flashes with pictures of whatever channel is on; the soundbar has been ripped away from the unit and rests on the floor. Picture frames lie shattered on the floor. The L-shaped couch is shredded, and the coffee table has a puddle of yellow fluid on it; I assume it's urine based on the ghastly smell.

"Steele," Zeile says. I turn around to see my captain looking the worse for wear.

"The place is trashed," I begin cautiously. "How could no one hear what was going on?"

"That's an understatement. As far as noise, the condo below hers is owned by a company overseas. No one seems actually to live there."

"Great. I don't know how to tell you what's out of place when this is an utter mess."

"I know you're working on no sleep, but even you know it isn't the common items I'm asking about. We've been collecting samples throughout, dusting for fingerprints, and what have you. I need you to tell me how it was before. Then, I need you to assist in going through her personal items. I don't need anyone going through her . . . unmentionables out of respect for the victim."

"I appreciate that, Cap. I don't think the perp got that memo," I finish as the captain hands me a pair of gloves that I snap on with practiced ease.

Without saying another word, I walk through the room, crunching on small pieces of leftover glass as I go. The once-neat shelving unit near the television housed movies, photos, and books. Only the photos have been knocked to the floor. The rest of the items remain untouched, clean. Kneeling, I scan over the frames tossed on the ground: One of Hadley and Frankie in college. One of Victor, Hadley, Frankie, and me from her first movie premiere's red carpet. Another one of all of us at graduation. One of her, Frankie, Logan, and me at her recent awards ceremony. As I push them aside, a broken, empty frame grabs my attention.

"She had a photo of her and Logan in here. Frankie took it when we were in Central Park for our annual end-of-summer barbecue. It was a candid, just the two of them looking at one another."

"Okay, what else?"

I wish I could remove all of the images from their frames and bring them home for Hadley. I'm sure it would help her feel better, but I'll have to wait until forensics has cleared everything. Sadly, it could also be a reminder of her loss. I turn my attention to her master bedroom. I wonder how far the perp went to violate her there.

The room is cleaner than the others, almost too clean, pure and untouched as if reverence was shared here. I don't know whether to be relieved or more concerned. I doubt any stalker would leave the most tantalizing room alone. Something had to have been touched, and I dread the answer, even though I have an inkling as to what it is.

Walking in behind me, Zeile breaks the silence. "The bedroom was like this when security gave us access. I wanted to wait until you got here and surveyed everything before the techs came in."

"The place is almost immaculate, but they're not stupid. You don't destroy the rest of the place and leave one room alone. Not unless you're trying to leave a message . . ." My eyes land on the top dresser drawer sticking out slightly more than the others. My gloved hands pull the blackish-brown dresser drawer open slowly. The bile in my stomach begins to bubble up to my esophagus. Hadley's bras, underwear, and lingerie have been rifled through. One can assume some pieces are missing. Looking around the room, I stare at the bed. The down comforter is perfectly spread out over the mattress. That isn't like Hadley at all.

"As we feared, he helped himself to some personal items." Zeile's voice is laced with disgust as he speaks from behind me.

"She always has the comforter on her side of the bed." The words fall out of my mouth mindlessly.

"Excuse me?" Zeile asks.

"Hadley's always cold at night. Logan runs hot, so he kicks the covers off. So, Hadley just started making the bed with the comforter hanging lower on her side. That way Logan didn't have as much to toss her way."

"I don't understand what the reference is here, Steele."

"They made the bed perfectly." I swallow the acid burning my throat. "Make sure they take the sheets," I finish before looking over to the balcony. "Hadley said they must have come in through a window since her bars were cut. I don't see any barriers on this side of the condo."

"The other side has bars near the fire escape. The window near the fire escape has a safety latch inside. It's designed to set off a silent alarm if opened."

"Could they access the interior from those cut bars?"

"Theoretically, yes, but doubtful. Maintenance says all the bars were to be replaced in the coming year with newer ones that were less obstructive. It seems like age, rust, and shoddy installation back in the day led them to break. Techs made molds of the ends, but it didn't look like any tool marks were present. We'll have to wait to find out more." Zeile stops for a second, and I can see him carefully planning out his words.

"Just say it."

"Considering the alarm systems and security downstairs . . ." he begins.

"She wasn't home at the time, Cap."

"True, but I'm sure someone in a different unit was. It's not uncommon for other residents to buzz people in thinking it's a delivery for them or their takeout. So, the bigger question for me is how did they have her key and alarm code?"

"They had to have been planning this for a very long time."

"Yes, which means Ms. Moreno—"

"She should be at a safe house."

"We both know that would be useless, Steele. Ms. Moreno is a public figure and will insist on working. We'd have to move her every night, and that is not an option."

"I'll have to talk to Frankie about it. We have Chase."

"I understand, and I normally wouldn't even consider it, but she is safer with you than with people I don't know."

Ignoring the ramifications of the question, I shoot a text off to Frankie, asking about the situation. After that, I scan the room one final time. The cleanliness, the perfect symmetry of it all—it's like a shrine with one focal point. Whoever they are might suffer from obsessive-compulsive disorder, but the mess outside would have tortured them. Nothing else explains the scene of her bedroom though.

"How's the other bedroom?"

"Set up as an office. Papers are strewn around the floor, but for the most part, it looks clean. It could have been staged to make this stand out more. Whoever did this wanted us to see this for what it is."

"Dominance and ownership. They feel they have it; Hadley didn't agree."

Briskly turning around, I walk to the master bathroom and push the door open gingerly. The missing photo of Logan and Hadley from the living room lay in a sink full of water. Logan's face is scratched out to the point of creating a hole in the picture. Dark red lipstick writing reflects at me from the mirror.

"*Vos es meus.*" The words fall out of my mouth with a perfect accent from my Catholic School days.

"What does it mean?"

"Loosely . . . *you are mine.*"

The words hang in the air between us for a few moments, the gravity of the case pressing further and further into our beings. The evidence shows an obsessed individual who has reached the point of violence, but they appear to be more intelligent than the stalkers I've seen in the past.

I lower my eyes from the window and back to the scratched-out face in the photo. The love of my friend's life. The one initially who saw her as a fan, but later on as an individual. The one person who never judged her for the job she chose or cared about her money. The geeky tech who asked ahead of time for videogame nights with his friends to ensure he wouldn't miss her important moments. The man who . . . I turn and look at Zeile.

"Where's Logan?"

Chapter Two

My cell phone once again goes to Logan's voicemail as we speed through the streets during morning rush hour. I've tried his landline as well as his social media accounts. The silence is deafening and raises the level of concern each time he doesn't answer. The trip to Brooklyn shouldn't be a long one, but with traffic and people having no place to move their cars, the drive might be too long.

Will Everts looks over at me and I dial the same number again. The speakerphone fills the sedan with the sound of ringing, which is barely audible over the sirens. Will, my partner for the last four years and a former Marine, cuts down a side street. The tires squeal as I hold on to the dash for support. Considering all the twists and turns, I assume he knows the area very well.

"Hi, you've reached Logan. I'm away from my phone . . ." the message begins before I hang up and dial the landline. Once again, the car is filled with the sound of ringing.

On the Brooklyn Bridge, cars squeeze to the right as we slowly pass one at a time. People biking or walking in the center turn to see where the noise is coming from. Some cover their ears as we pass. Like any human nature response, they're probably wondering where we're off to in such a rush. Like *schadenfreude*, the thoughts of a gruesome car accident, shooting, robbery, or fire might pop into their minds. They'll thank the heavens it's not them before offering thoughts and prayers to the victims. These are the same people that beg for calm but thrive in calamity.

"We're almost there," Will shouts over the screech of sirens blaring out from our car. "Keep trying," he adds as a different voicemail message plays.

Fruitless or not, I dial Logan's cell phone again. Maybe he was in the shower during my previous calls. Maybe he set everything to *Do Not Disturb* so the ringer wouldn't go off. There could be any number of reasons he's not answering his phones this early in the morning. I can think of a myriad of them, including the one where Logan's body is cold on the floor. I shake the vision from my mind as voicemail picks up again. Disconnecting the call, I place my cell back in the holster. Continuing to call when we're almost there is just causing more anxiety for the two of us.

"I swear to God if he's got noise-canceling headphones on in an all-night gaming binge, I will destroy that Xbox in front of him!" Will says, his voice cracking slightly. The Marine is showing his breaking point as his emotions get the better of him. We've all been there. We can't lose another one of our own. We're not ready to face that again.

"Cap call ahead?" I ask, trying to focus on the task at hand.

"Yeah, the super is waiting for us out front."

Once again, the tires squeal as Will rounds the corner onto Logan's block. I shut the sirens off but leave the lights flashing. Will pulls into a spot at an angle behind another car. The end of the sedan sticks out into the narrow street with cars parked on both sides. The two of us jump out of the car and rush up to an older Hispanic male in paint-covered khaki cargo pants in front of Logan's place.

"You the police?" he asks since we're both in plain clothes. Will flashes his badge, and the man quickly opens both doors. The cramped little foyer, with a warped staircase on the right and resident mailboxes beneath, it looks dank and old.

"Pre-World War II building, so the elevator is slow," the super says, pushing the button more than once.

Will says nothing but turns to the stairs and begins taking them two at a time. I hear him hit the first landing as he continues his journey to the third floor. His boots echo every time his foot hits a step.

The elevator dings, notifying its arrival, and the door shakily opens. Listening carefully, I'm sure Will is already on the third floor. The super hits three and everything rattles. I grab hold of the handle and focus on Logan, not the vibration of this antiquated box. Once the doors open again, I quickly make a right, heading for apartment thirty-six. People walk past me in their work attire before heading down the stairs quickly. Down the hallway, Will is knocking on doors and talking to other residents.

"I want you to stay here and give me the key," I say to the super. "Please, it's for your safety."

"My boss . . ."

"We will deal with the landlord if necessary," I answer quickly.

Reluctantly, he holds out a ring of keys, the one I need between his two fingers. I grab them and mouth "thank you" before rushing down the hall to meet my partner.

"I got the family in the apartment across from him to leave early, but the one next door refuses to leave. At least we can block this off," Will says, clearly out of breath.

He presses his ear firmly to the metal door. We don't know the situation inside the apartment, and we need to be careful. I pull out my service weapon and wait for his direction.

"Anything?" I lower my voice.

"Nothing." Will leans back and pulls out his revolver. I slide the key into the top lock and slowly open it. I place it in the lower lock and look over to Will. "Door opens to the left, blocking the living area," he says. "You go in first and head right, clear the kitchen. I'll check the bathroom quickly before we meet in the living room. Okay?"

Will's hand replaces mine as he turns the key slowly, trying to minimize the noise. The sound of the light switch hits our ears, and his grip switches to the doorknob. He opens the door, and I move directly inside and to the right. Will leaves the door open, protecting our backs, as he checks the main bathroom. In seconds, both rooms clear, we come back to the small entryway. Holding his gun out in front of him, Will pushes the door open fully.

The room is unlit, except for the sun peeking through the back windows. The main illumination comes from the television screen displaying a video game's main menu screen across the sixty inches of real estate. A glimpse of the curved headband of his gaming headphones is visible just above the couch.

Almost painfully slow, we round the couch. Logan rests there, hunched over, with his eyes firmly shut. Will moves toward his prone form, checking for a pulse. I open the bedroom door and ensure the place is truly clear of the perpetrator. Finding the room and its closets empty, I holster my weapon and move back to the living room.

"There's a pulse, but it's really weak."

Logan's thumbs twitch on the controller, moving the thumb sticks a little bit. Will grabs his cell phone and quickly dials emergency services.

"Nine-one-one, what's your emergency?"

"This is Detective Will Everts," I hear as his voice fades out in the background.

"Tell them he's unconscious, breathing is shallow, and his bottom lip is swollen," I say without thinking. Hearing a slight wheeze, I pray I'm doing the right thing by moving him. Sliding Logan to the floor, I place him on his left side.

"Any blood?" Will asks me.

"None that I can see," I answer quickly. I bend his right leg to a ninety-degree angle, his left arm at the same angle to prevent him from rolling over and his right arm bent under his chin. His breathing is still shallow and strained, but if he regurgitates anything, it won't choke him to death.

"They're one minute out," Will says, standing above me and Logan. "You moved him."

"Yeah . . . CPR's recovery position."

"Yeah, anything helps," he tosses out, the helpless feeling evident in his voice and on his face. "I'll go make sure the elevator's there and waiting." He turns and rushes out the door, leaving me alone with Logan. I sit on the floor, rubbing his back, unsure of what else I can do.

The place looks clean, with no evidence of a break-in. The door was locked, so there was no forced entry. The windows are closed. A remote control rests by his beer on the coffee table, a small personal pizza box from a local shop near the drink. Nothing else is out of the ordinary. My thoughts break when the sound of heavy footfalls reaches my ears. Will, followed by two paramedics, push inside the small apartment. Mindlessly, I stand and move out of their way.

"Allergies?" a muscular paramedic with salt-and-pepper hair asks us as he gets an IV into Logan's arm.

"Not that we know of," Will answers. The paramedic injects something into the IV, and Logan's breathing instantly sounds better, but not great.

"We need to call Hadley; she'll know more."

"Take the car and go get her. Meet us at the hospital."

"Go to Bellevue," Will answers quickly.

"Sir . . ." the heavier but younger-looking paramedic begins.

"It's the only place he trusts. We're close enough; stabilize him and go there," Will presses.

"He could die in transport."

"He could die on the floor. Just fucking take him to the hospital he prefers," I say before alarms fill the room.

"Pulse ox is low. We need to intubate, but his throat is swollen. Call it in." The other paramedic pushes past me and grabs the gurney sitting in the hallway.

"Detective, we're going to take your friend to Bellevue," he says bluntly, then turns his attention to Will. "You riding with us?" he asks as they transfer Logan and quickly strap him down to the bed.

"Yes."

"Then let's go."

The two rush the gurney out the door and down the hall. Without thinking, I lock the door behind us. Maybe it was to preserve the crime scene. It could have been a silly thing to do, but having any mindless activity to do helps keep me sane.

***

The ride to pick up Hadley before heading to the hospital was relatively quick. Using all the shortcuts I could, I was at my house in minutes, helping my ashen-faced friend into the car. Sirens were blasting all the way to the hospital, and we parked in the employee area with permission. Hadley was out of my car before I cut the engine and wanted to rush inside—until she realized she had no clue where to go.

Now inside, we sit in wood chairs with barely enough padding for a ten-minute wait, let alone hours, and wait for the doctors to come back. They had asked Will a hundred questions upon their arrival, most of which he couldn't answer, but he wasn't next of kin or a medical proxy. No one knew who his advocate was until Hadley walked in purposefully. She handed the nurse a copy of the medical proxy paperwork and insisted nothing else was to occur without her knowledge. I don't even remember her grabbing the files when I stopped by.

Soft music plays overhead. It's meant to be calming, but the more I shift from hip to hip, the more annoying everything becomes. It's during these moments of hypersensitivity that panic rises within me. It's when the fear crawls up my legs like a spider, taking its time before hitting my chest cavity with a full-fledged panic attack. Logan is younger than the majority of the team. He's got his whole life ahead of him. He's got Hadley, and together they have a real shot at happiness.

We both work in a field with a high mortality rate. Remove the dangerous situations with weapons or disturbed persons. Just look at the mental, emotional, and physical toll the positions tax your body with every day. We're the first line of defense from the horrors of humankind, but we absorb the negative we shield you from. Like in any war, the first line is expendable. Money is funneled away from our healthcare or retirement packages. Governments use our names to get elected. One bad apple in the bunch causes all their deleterious actions to rain down on us all. Yet, we all still willingly go to work every day. It may be our last, but we never expect it when it comes.

"Any updates?" she asks, waking up from a short, stress-induced nap. She looks around, her left hand squeezing mine tightly. "They should be keeping me abreast of the situation."

"They took him in a little while ago. Once someone has more information, they'll come and tell us. Until then, we have to wait." I try to calm her down, but I can see my words fall on deaf ears.

"Not good enough. I want to speak to someone right now!" Hadley releases my hand and marches over to the employee behind a small desk. "I need to know what's going on with Logan Pevy."

"Ma'am . . ."

"I'm Hadley Moreno, his medical proxy. Someone was supposed to update me with his progress, but no one has. Can you please find out what the hell is going on?"

"Ms. Moreno, I can tell you they are in the OR right now, but I don't have any information beyond that. I can make a call and see if someone will come out and speak to you," the woman says, trying to calm Hadley.

I'm not sure if it's working. Frankie would know how to help Hadley, but she's with Chase right now.

"Please do that." She quickly spins around to face me. "Jasmine, why aren't they telling me anything. They promised . . . he promised . . . it was just game night . . ." Her body systematically begins breaking down as tears threaten to drop down her cheeks.

The doors to the inner workings of the hospital buzz open and Captain Zeile walks out. "Steele" he begins, looking at me before he notices Hadley next to me. It's as if her body, once allowing itself to grieve, immediately places all the walls back in place to keep her poised and ready.

"Ms. Moreno, I'm glad you're here. We have a more comfortable room in which to wait out the surgery. I've spoken to several doctors, and they will be periodically checking in on Logan and reporting to that room."

"Cap?" I ask, wondering how he managed this.

"A very close friend is running the ward tonight," he whispers to me. "Ms. Moreno should have some privacy when the news of Mr. Pevy's attack hits the news. We can only control the crowd for so long, and this area is not secure. My friend and I agreed moving Ms. Moreno into a private room would be best for all parties involved."

The captain leads us back through the hospital doors and down a long hallway before taking a right and then a quick left. If I leave, I doubt I'll find this room again. He stops in front of an Employees Only sign and swipes a keycard. It clicks open, and he holds the door for everyone to walk inside.

"Ms. Moreno, this is an employee lounge, but no one will be using this one until further notice. The coffee machine and hot water are available to use, but we will have to bring food in. You just let any officer know what you'd like and we'll ensure it's brought in. Okay?"

"Yes, thank you. Have they said anything to you?"

"No. I know it's been a while, but no news is better than bad news." He recites the adage that my mother would tell me when my oma was in the hospital after a head injury.

"Take care of her," he says to me before heading to the door. "Will is briefing several officers outside. No one will get in this room without proper authorization. In the meantime, I've got the crime scene unit ripping apart Logan's apartment. I'll check in with you later."

"Thanks, Cap. Keep me posted."

And just like that, he's gone. The door closes with a soft click, and the noises of the ward disappear. The intimate room has a table in the middle and comfortable-looking couches along two walls, desks on another wall, and the food area on the last one. The coffee maker, complete with Keurig servings of tea, coffee, and hot chocolate, rests on the counter with a dormitory fridge underneath it.

Hadley looks smaller than I've ever seen her, knees to her chest, hands wrapped around them, rocking back and forth on one of the couches.

"I don't understand what happened." She breathes. "Tell me what happened."

"Hadley. . ."

"I know you told me at the house, but I didn't hear you. Please, go through it again slowly."

"Okay. Cap called me to the apartment. We went through everything, and it hit me that we hadn't heard from Logan all night. If you were in trouble, he was always the first call."

"But it was game night, and he missed the last one, so I didn't want to bother him." She pauses and covers her mouth quickly. "Oh my God, if I had called him, maybe he wouldn't have gotten attacked. Maybe he'd be at your house holding me. Jasmine, what did I do?"

"You did nothing wrong. This isn't on you at all, Had. Someone hurt the man you love, not you. We can't worry about 'maybes' or 'what-ifs.' We have to focus on the right now."

"I'll try," she says. She sniffles and places her hand back around her knee. Tears freely roll down her face as the weight of the day slides loose. "What happened when you got to the building?"

"Will ran up the stairs, and I took the elevator with the super. We opened the door and cleared the kitchen and bathroom before entering the living room, as per procedure. While Will checked on Logan, I cleared the bedroom."

"Was he conscious?"

"No. His hands were on the controller, headset on, and his thumbs were moving like he was still playing *Borderlands*."

"Was he breathing?"

"Weakly. Will called for the ambulance while I put him in the recovery position."

"Did he ever wake up while you were with him?"

"No."

She pauses, looking out the windows to the world outside. "I thought he'd be safer at home than with me. I know he has a weekly standing game night with Will and Chase, but he hasn't enjoyed a game night with his college buddies in so long. I figured he'd be . . . all to make sure I was safe. He knew about the letters, the calls—all of it. It was too close, you know? I thought, 'If he's at home, he's not in harm's way.' He doesn't have a target on his back because of me. Stupid, right?"

"Not at all. It's human nature to protect the ones you love." I sit down next to her, throwing my arm around her shoulders. She uncoils herself and curls into my side. I've seen Hadley do this every time she failed to get a part or if a bad review came in.

"Did he know he was . . . Did he feel any pain? I mean . . ." Her breathing escalates. Her short breaths hiccup as tears pool against my shirt, and I wrap my other arm around her, pulling her in close.

"Had, you need to slow your breathing for me, okay? Deep breaths." With my right hand, I rub small circles on her back, trying to calm her anxiety. "In and out. Just focus on my breathing, okay?"

"Talk to me," she whispers between breaths.

"About what?"

"Anything."

"Okay . . . Gino Reyes, my first partner when I became a detective, we were working on the Carnation Killer Case together. You remember the one we just solved?"

She nods her head.

"Yeah, well, he told me he preferred cases that were easier to process mentally and paperwork-wise. He'd always say, *'Steele, you had a perp, you had a victim, and you had a solution. Pretty cut and dry. Nowadays, every case is all gray, like no-fault car insurance. Drives me crazy.'* Anyway, he used to work out on Long Island as a beat cop before he transferred to the city. Gino got the worst calls all day long. Random car accidents and a bunch of other shit. Don't get me started on the time a couple of kids set the cops' favorite diner on fire. He ranted about 'those little shits' for weeks. He told me about this older man in Plainview who would constantly call them about people walking dogs in front of his house. Something about them allowing the dog to pee on his grass."

"It's his property . . ."

"Yeah, the guy owns it, but he would threaten every person who walked by. It didn't matter if they were in the street following the law, either. He made the town give him street signs to put on the stop sign at the intersection. He scared his elderly neighbors so often with their senior dog that they called inquiring about a restraining order. Young kids would cross the street with their dogs because he'd terrify them. The grumpy old man would rant, rave, and scream at whoever was by his house. This real piece of work would scream from his wicker chair on the front porch. One day, Gino gets a call from that guy's address. He shows up with his partner, and the guy's lying on his back, twitching on the front lawn. There's a good number of neighbors around, all on the street beyond the curb. Gino goes to help while his partner calls an ambulance."

"Let me guess: cell phones out recording instead of assisting?"

"Hell no. This was before pagers even existed, Hadley, forget about a cell phone." I smile slightly. Her reactions and full voice tell me her breathing is back to normal, and her brain is focusing on something else.

"The guy ends up dying from a heart attack right in the center of his front lawn. Paramedics show up, declare it, and cover the body while they wait for the coroner. Gino and his partner start interviewing all the people in the street. It turns out he stormed out of his house toward two young women walking their little nothing of a dog well inside the street. Witnesses said the girls tried to walk away, laugh it off or whatnot, but he kept coming after them, and the women were frightened.

"Neighbors, hearing the usual commotion, had had enough. They come out and defend the two girls. This enrages the old man, and he starts screaming at them all and runs back in and calls the police. He yells into the phone, hangs up, sprints back into the yard, and continues huffing and puffing at the crowd. After a minute or two more of screaming about the law and his lawn, the guy keels over, grabbing his chest."

Hadley leans back slightly, her breathing now fully under control. Her head rests on my shoulder as I keep a comforting hold on her.

"The neighbors all admitted to not helping the man, regardless of the Good Samaritan laws. Every single one of them said they respected the man's wishes and remained off his lawn at all times. Gino would tell it better than I did, but he'd finish by telling me Karma fed that man a full sandwich that day. The old guy was a vile neighbor and an irritation to police and the community. He paid the ultimate price for it."

"Don't you think the neighbors were wrong? I mean, they should have helped."

"Truthfully, I don't know. Here's a guy who spent his life making other people's lives hell. How would they know if he would accept help? Maybe that man would have attacked them for walking on his property; he'd done it before. The first rule of thumb is to make sure the place is safe for you to assist. In this case, I'd say it wasn't."

"Of all the things you could have told me about, why this one?"

"Two reasons: One, because when you're going through something, it's never black-and-white. Two, it's a simple reminder that karma is a real bitch and always gets her revenge. This stalker will eat a big plate of it."

"Do you think they hurt Logan?"

"I—"

"Please don't lie to me."

"It's too convenient for my taste. I can't say for sure, though. We don't know what's wrong with Logan yet."

"He can't die, Jazz. I need him. He grounds me, you know?" She closes her eyes and leans back, facing the ceiling. "I love him; he needs to stay with me."

Her body begins to shake, and more tears roll down her face and onto her shirt. "I know, Had. I know."

"Ms. Moreno?" A woman whom I assume is the doctor stands with the door slightly ajar.

Hadley jumps up and stands at attention. Her right hand reaches back for emotional support. My hand clasps hers as the doctor walks forward, lowering her voice so I can't hear their private conversation.

After a minute, the doc leaves, and Hadley remains there, squeezing my hand as if her life depends on it. She turns, and I see the silent tears rolling down her face. Instantly, I'm on my feet, pulling her into my arms. Her body shakes violently as her arms squeeze the air out of my lungs. I don't know what the doctor shared with her, but in my experience with hospitals, tears are never good.

Chapter Three

The small space in the basement is our new office, or holding pen as we affectionately call it. The former storage unit still has old file cabinets against the north wall. They're empty, waiting for new files to be stored in them, but scratches and rust indicate their age. Four metal desks from decades gone by rest in a square in the middle. A counter follows along the south wall, complete with a small apartment-sized fridge at the end. An old coffee machine, which Captain Zeile donated to our workspace, and a microwave Will insisted we need rest on top. Mounted on the west wall is a massive, brand-new whiteboard.

The thick tension in the room threatens to choke the air from my lungs. As I exit the elevator into the musty office, Will and Sydney Locke sit at their desks looking through some papers. The newest member of our team, Sydney filled in for Will on our last case and never left.

"News?" Will asks and looks up from his desk, hopeful.

"They've placed Logan in a medically induced coma. Frankie's with Had now, and Cap has unis there to keep the unauthorized out. They'll let us know if anything changes, for better or worse."

"How's she holding up?" Sydney asks as she stands and goes to brew herself a cup of coffee.

"As well as can be expected," I say, walking over to the desk with my nameplate on it. "Did Cap decide if he's going to use that, or can we start piling stuff on it now?" I point to the empty desk across from Sydney.

"Cap is staying in his office. That's for the liaison we have with the FBI," Sydney answers as she loads the top of the coffee maker.

"Who would subject themselves to the dungeon to work with the department of misfit toys?" The sarcasm rolls off my tongue with practiced ease.

"The agent you referred me to with the Keets case. Agent Karina Marlow? She's damn good," Sydney says.

Agent Karina Marlow had been essential in ending Irving Garrison's criminal career once and for all—the rise and fall of a prominent businessman dealing in human trafficking, drugs, and other nefarious activities. Without Marlow and the FBI, we wouldn't have been able to bring down everyone in the web—judges, and politicians alike.

After her return to Seattle, we have remained in frequent contact. During all our conversations, her move to our city department never came up. Uprooting her children during the school year would have been overly disruptive. Marlow would never do that without a substantial reason. Inquiring about it will have to wait; we've got more important things to handle.

"Anything back from either apartment?" I ask.

"Nothing conclusive," Sydney begins. "So far, we've only managed to exclude some fingerprints from those collected. Mostly, Logan's and Hadley's. They're currently running the rest of you to remove those from the collection. Then they'll run it through CODIS. No ETA on when it'll be done." Sydney walks back over to her desk, her cup filled with the freshly brewed coffee. She sits down and leans back in her chair, showing off her newly purchased and fashionable but still sensible boots.

"Anything else?" I ask, tossing my jacket on the back of my chair.

Will says, "Teams are still on site. We got lucky that prints were brought back and cataloged this quickly."

"What about the pizza we found near Logan?"

"Being tested," he says. "Steele, you know all of this takes time. Lillian knows to push our stuff to the front of the line as much as possible. Everyone's doing the best they can, given the circumstances."

"I understand. I was hoping for any little kernel to work on while we wait for updates from the hospital. You know we'll all go crazy if we just sit here."

During our conversation, I hadn't noticed Dr. Victor Hayes, our coroner and resident fashion guide, walk in from the stairs entrance with a banker's box in his hands. The morgue, where Victor has wild conversations with the dead, is directly above us. Victor wouldn't stop laughing that we're below the dead. No one else got the joke.

"Logan's been paying attention to her fan mail," Victor says. "I called her agent and asked for more. He dropped it off a little while ago." He's wearing dark slacks and a blue button-down shirt and shifting from foot to foot in his designer shoes. "I should have asked first, but I needed something to do. I couldn't wait for him to end up on my table. I don't want that."

Victor walks over to our square and drops the box on Marlow's empty desk. "Her agent mentioned the studio possibly getting more. Told him to get whatever he could."

"Thanks, Vic," I say as Will and Sydney grab a handful of letters each.

"You might want to wear those," Victor says and points to a small box of medical gloves in the corner. "Dot our i's and cross our t's," he finishes, referencing the book of regulations we all follow when dealing with evidence.

The other two glove up without saying a word. Victor reaches over, grabs the box, and holds it out for me. Taking two, I fight to get my hands in the small blue mitts. The coroner just stands there, waiting for someone to say anything or give him direction.

"Office quiet?" I ask.

"All caught up," he says.

"Dig in," I say, grabbing a stack of letters and sitting down at my desk. Victor gives a slight smile as he snaps on a pair of gloves with expert precision. Taking his place at Marlow's desk, he immediately opens a letter.

I grab my car keys out of my jacket and flip open the old small pocketknife. The blade is just as sharp as the day it hung on my opa's keyring, then my mother's, and now mine. It quickly slices the envelope with ease. Sliding the letter out and unfolding it, the first thing I notice is the penmanship: small, bubbly letters with wild loops on the Y's and G's throughout the message. The words of adoration and thanks pour off the page with sincerity. A young teen, looking up to my friend like a beacon of hope—someone who isn't afraid to take risks with her career, regardless of Hollywood's plans for her. It's a lovely letter, but it's obviously not who I'm looking for.

I drop it on the left half of my desk, starting a pile of exclusions. Ripping open the next one, I'm immediately repulsed by images of a man's penis with some grotesque, hand-drawn positions.

"I wish this was illegal." I hold out the photos to show my colleagues. They groan their displeasure as they turn back to their letters. Will empties his small metal inbox tray and drops it at the center of the four corners of our desks.

"Suspicious pile for the district attorney. I'd start with that one." He points to my letter with the attached photos. I paperclip them together before dropping the entire thing into the container.

"If I wasn't gay before . . ."

"Technically, you weren't," Sydney says. "Until you were, of course."

"Just keep reading," I answer, shaking my head.

Sydney smirks as she turns her attention back to the mountain of letters. I deftly open another one. The words all blend together: *"you're amazing," "I love you," "thank you for being such a role model."* Harmless fans were writing to their idol, hoping for a glimmer of a connection.

One after another, I find musings of children with their stick figure drawings, teenagers with beautiful fan art, and adults with simple words of thanks. The innocent individuals who say their piece and hope Hadley reads it. Now, their words are being read by foreign eyes because of one lunatic's actions, letters discarded to a pile Hadley will most likely never see. Her agents should take over her interactions to keep her safe.

After six handfuls, my eyes feel the strain of scanning so many documents. Most are handwritten, which surprised me. The rest are typed with a signature at the bottom like a business endeavor. The last one in my stack starts like all the rest. *Dear Hadley, I find you beyond talented. Your talent is only surpassed by your kindness . . . but you seem to waste it on so many people who aren't as deserving as I am.*

Like tiny little soldiers standing at attention, the hairs on my neck rise with small goose bumps. As I continue reading, the feeling migrates down my body to my toes. His words are not outright threatening, but the tone creeps me out. Suspicious, yes. Stalker, maybe. Disturbing, one hundred percent.

"There are so many nights I dream of you. The way you feel in my arms, against my lips, beneath me, begging for more. I know you need that boy as a diversion from our love. It's understandable, but I think we need to come clean now. I love you and you love me too. You said so yourself at our photo op at Comic-Con. I know you wouldn't have said it if you didn't mean it." The letter goes on, and I stop reading to prevent my stomach from rolling any more than it already is.

"I've got a hit." I hand Will the letter, and his eyes scan through the page systematically. The muscles in his jaw flex, relax, then flex again. I can only imagine what he thinks as he reads. His children have been around Hadley quite often. We're a hodgepodge of a family, after all. His daughters spend countless hours scanning magazines, laughing over quizzes and boys. Hadley rose to the occasion of being an aunt to any one of our kids. Now, it's becoming clear to all of us how dangerous the entertainment business is.

The Garrison case and his unnatural desire for Hadley felt like a one-time thing. This, it's real. It's a normal person on the street watching our kids go to school. He could be any face, any color, any religion . . . He might not even be a he at all.

"Hold my beer," Sydney adds, tossing another letter onto the pile.

"Mine too," Victor says.

After a few more minutes of opening letters, the suspicious pile continues to grow steadily. It's astounding to me how Hadley manages to work and be professional with all these fanatics running around. I want to be proud of her but also smack her silly for not having a bodyguard. As we scrape the bottom of the box, the tray is overflowing with options, and we've only just scratched the surface.

"How many?" Will asks, staring at the pile.

"Last count, around sixty." Victor leans back in his chair, playing with a ring on his right hand.

"This is just the tip of the iceberg, isn't it?" I ask as fear leaches into my voice.

"I'm sure if we go through things, we'll find a pattern. Maybe the majority are all from one person," Sydney adds as she yawns and reaches for her now-cold coffee. "It could be a very manageable list."

"You said her agent was bringing more over?" Will asks as he stands and walks over to the coffee machine. Sydney holds her mug up in the air, begging for a refill. "My eyes are blurry from deciphering handwriting." Will finishes filling Sydney's mug before returning to his own.

"Mine too, but this box doesn't even include emails, social media comments, direct messages, or whatever else. There's got to be a way to sort through it all much faster than this." My words stop short of bringing Logan into the conversation. If he were here, we'd have some algorithm to filter everything through and narrow down. I never understood how he managed to do everything so quickly and flawlessly. Our team feels broken. Our team *is* broken.

The new gadget on my wrist starts vibrating incessantly with an alarm I don't remember setting. Tapping the screen, trying to turn it off, does nothing. Hitting buttons stops it from annoying me. Next time Frankie and Chase want to retire an old piece of equipment I like to use, I'll fight it. That Timex from high school still worked, fashion be damned.

"Hospital?" Will asks, and the rest of the team waits for me to answer.

"No, not them. Just a reminder I have an appointment."

"Everything okay?" Will continues to press a bit. He knows I carry things close to the vest when it comes to my health, but the man saved my life. I owe him honesty whenever I feel comfortable giving it. Right now, I don't. Vague answers it is.

"Yeah, nothing big." I pick up two letters and scan the visibly similar penmanship. "I can't believe people write anything by hand, let alone mail actual letters. Might work in our favor if Lil can get some analysis done."

"Just add it to her to-do list," Victor says with a slightly harsh tone. He's been dating Lillian for a while now, and I'm sure putting her under this amount of pressure doesn't make him happy.

Will cuts in before I can respond to Victor. "Go to your appointment. We can hold the fort until you get back."

"I'm good, got a ton of time." The words come out of my mouth as Will rolls my chair away from the desk with me on it. "Will . . ."

"Not asking." He once again cuts me off as my chair stops in front of the elevator doors. He pushes the up button, grabs my jacket, and holds it out to me.

"Seriously, I'm good," I say and laugh.

"Happy wife, happy life." He smirks.

"Frankie called you." He knows the truth.

"No. Our wives have apparently become best friends and share every-thing. I don't know if we should be happy or terrified at the prospect."

"Terrified. Trust me." I grab my leather jacket out of his hands as the elevator dings behind me. Stepping inside, I make a "call me" gesture at Victor, and he nods his head in response. The doors close and whisk me away to a city full of life outside. People are walking at a faster pace around those texting while ambulating about. The sun is shining and reflecting off all the sunglasses. I wonder how many of them are fake or covering up some internal pain with a smile right now. I'm envious of them. I place my black sunglasses on to block out the world; my resting bitch face comes on strong. I weave through to the judgmental crowds of the subway.

***

I don't like going places and talking with people I've never met. It's part of the job when interviewing witnesses or a suspect, but that's always about something else. Discussing oneself is a very different animal. Standing in front of a strange penthouse door on Central Park West, I'm more fascinated by the layers of brown paint slathered on the door than knocking. Excuses run through my mind to make a quick escape and avoid the one thing I swore I would never do. If it wasn't job-related, there would never be any reason to come to this place. Standing in the hallway of a building with overly inflated rent, I want to run. None of this is necessary. I'm strong. I can do this on my own.

The door opens before my body can catch up with my brain and vacate the premises.

"Detective Steele?"

"Dr. Jenette Preston?" I throw back nervously. She nods in response. "I was just . . ."

"Contemplating a quick exit?"

"No." I try but fail to convince her. "I promised Frankie I'd be here." Her dark eyes bore holes into me as a mother's would. "Maybe I was. Contemplating an exit."

"Well, you're here now, so come in."

Hands shoved deep in my jean's pockets—a defense mechanism I never grew out of—I walk inside and immediately start analyzing the woman's place. The hallway is painted white with small frames of ducks and other innocuous things. A door to the left is closed off from the visitors or patients who come in. Next to it is the kitchen with small, high-end appliances. I'd never fit Chase's food in that anemic fridge. The living room has top-of-the-line electronics and a leather loveseat with a matching chair. Everything about this place screams simple, and it's hard to get a read on who she is.

"I work from home, detective. I prefer not to broadcast everything about my personal life to my clientele."

"I wasn't—"

"You were, and you know it. Everyone in our field does it. We analyze everything to get a handle on a situation. You've got a psychology degree; it's impossible to turn off. It's our way of controlling an environment."

She walks to the second of another two doors on the right wall. Opening it, she waves me inside. A mahogany desk sits across the room with no chairs in front of it. Another leather loveseat and matching chair are to the left of me. A metal and glass coffee table settles in between. Disney coasters sit in the center, neatly stacked: *Ratatouille*. Chase loves that film. I walk to the window on the outside wall of the building and look out into the park.

"Would you like to sit?"

"Why don't you tell me about yourself," I counter.

"The first rule of psychology . . ."

"Never share personal details. I know."

"This is your time. How you use it is up to you, but I reserve the right not to answer."

"Where did you go to school?"

"Hofstra University for my Bachelors. C.W. Post for my doctorate. Columbia University for my residency."

"A lot of names and debt."

"A lot of hard work, scholarships, and chances gained while sleep was lost."

"Where did you go to high school?"

"I don't see the relevance."

"Where did you grow up?"

"I'm not going to play this game, detective. Some questions don't add to a conversation; they distract from the real reason you're here."

"My colleague and I routinely say, 'Happy wife, happy life.'" My fists clench in my pockets. Frankie knows how difficult this place is for me.

"Yes, Dr. Ryan is concerned about you. She also explicitly stated that our meetings be under the umbrella of patient privilege. No one will know of your visits unless you are a danger to yourself or others."

"You run the practice out of your house, doc. People can find out."

"I only see specific clients here. Otherwise, they come to my office in Midtown. You can easily defer these meetings as business-related. I am bound by confidentiality; you aren't."

"You remind me of my father; you have an answer or excuse for everything."

"And I'm old enough to have heard them all. Would you like to talk about your father?"

"Uh, no." I continue scanning the scene below.

Wave after wave of cars roll by on the street, oblivious to the life above it. People are wandering into the park seeking the serenity hidden within, unaware I'm watching them.

"You think any of them are having a bad day?" I ask.

"Who? The people out there? Statistically speaking, yes."

"Every day we walk by someone, bump them, don't say thank you, ignore them with music . . . We push each other further away. Maybe acknowledging someone with a smile could keep them from killing themselves. Just saying hello might convince someone that they matter, you know? Like we don't care what color, religion, or whatever. You're just a person standing next to me at Starbucks."

"That's rather insightful." The leather creaks as Jenette sits on the loveseat across from me. Her hair cascades down her shoulders, the tight black ringlets highlighted by streaks of gray. Her dark skin and full-bodied frame give her a warm, motherly feel. Her brown eyes pull at my soul. It feels as if they could see right through my Cancer crab shell and into my very being. It is both comforting and unnerving.

"Not really. It's logical."

"Do you feel others see it as you do?"

"No." I turn from the window and walk around to fall into the chair across from her. "If they did, we wouldn't want to kill each other for the adjectives that describe what we are. We'd be more accepting of humanity as a diverse creation instead of using differences to divide us."

"That bothers you."

"I'm a cop. Of course it does."

"You're a detective, not just any cop. Frankie tells me you're part of an experimental division?"

"It's common in other cities actually; we just hadn't had one in our department. No big deal."

"Yet only a select few were chosen for it."

"I think it was that or a suspension." The fake laugh erupts out of my chest as a pure defense mechanism. My right leg bounces consistently, my boot squeaking against the wood floors. "If we're gonna do this, I need you to be a pseudofriend more than a doc."

"That's not—"

"Doc, I'm a cop. If I want to find shit out about you, I only need to log in. It's called a rapport. We both know the concept, so humor me, okay? Walls of silence and all that shit—not for me. I can't handle this 'talk about yourself' crap. It's not me. I help people."

"You also fill in the silence."

"Yeah, it's a nervous habit."

She leans back on the couch and crosses her legs. Her comfortably stylish shoes hang from her toes, heels free to breathe the recirculated air. It's then she allows me to take her in fully. Fashionable, but not label-heavy clothing loosely fits around her frame. She's not muscular nor obese, but the way she leans back screams pride, respect, and power. She exudes these strong features but still maintains this calm demeanor that makes her feel safe. It's an odd combination, but I assume it's out of necessity.

"You done?"

Sitting upright in the chair, I nod in response instead of verbalizing my thoughts.

"And? What are your conclusions?"

"I don't think you hide your life from the walls for safety. You don't show much of anything. Your stance shows power, confidence, and demands respect. Yet, you don't wear clothing to match it. You haven't colored those pesky white hairs to look younger. Yet, you take care of your skin, you have a clean place, and you have good hygiene. You do all of that for the outside world."

"Which means what to you, detective?"

"Considering your place as well, I would say you are a woman who doesn't want the world to know her strengths or weaknesses. You want to come off as powerful and fit within society, but you won't spend like it. Most people who fit that mold have come from a time when money was scarce. Beyond that, you have a quality about you in this room. One that makes people want to talk and feel safe. If they asked for a hug, I think you would indulge them if it helped. A true dichotomy between the two sides. One for outside that door, and the other for those who need help or family."

"It's funny how much you can read from just listening to the universe."

"Was I close?"

"Closer than most. You, on the other hand, are an enigma. You scream power. Even slumped in a chair, your hands clenched, the tension in your shoulders. You are always in control and never wish to be viewed otherwise. Beyond that, you're blank—eyes hidden behind a shield. Expressions, simple movements, everything is calculated. Why don't you want to broadcast who you are to the world, detective?"

"That's simple. If I do, people can die."

"I doubt it's that direct."

I want to reply, but I can't. She's correct in her assumption, but to agree is to accept that I cannot control everything around me. To say that allows the insecurities of my life to come roaring back in my mind. And that's not for today. Maybe in the future, but not now.

"Nothing is, but yet it can be." The vague answer hangs in the air between us. Silence follows. Her eyes search mine for further answers or guidance on where to go next.

The quiet is the worst part of my life. I keep flashing back to when Frankie dragged me to yoga classes for a month. She would fall asleep, sometimes snoring when we were finishing up. I would stare at the ceiling, count the cracks, and wonder if they leaked. Frankie would refuse to speak with me the entire class. She would argue that yoga was to clear all thoughts away, so conversations were to be internal. I had a lot of fights with her in my head during those times.

But the silence was effective. It forced me to internalize. Just like Jenette is doing now. She sits there comfortably, waiting for me to open the line of communication in a different direction. It's a standoff with a shrink that a patient will usually lose. But I'm not like everyone else, and right now, the silence doesn't bother me one bit.

Chapter Four

Hospitals are a city unto themselves. They've got their governing body that seemingly puts the value of a dollar over that of a life. If you follow the hierarchy, you see a similar concept to a cruise ship or a country's government. And, like a city, they breed diseases and death. Then you get the bill for the privilege of dying there.

That's partially why I hate this place. It screams death to me with every announcement overhead. The nurses rush by to try and save a human as the calculators continue to add. It's a cold place. People are tired, overworked, and you are no different than the family member in the next bed over. It's a business more than healthcare.

Then again, Hadley has the ability to push her weight around, and she has a name and a bank account to back it up. Just by virtue of her career path and a ton of hard work. Not bad for a mixed-race brat from the Bronx. It makes it a little more tolerable. A little more.

"I brought you some coffee," I say.

Frankie Ryan, a well-known psychologist in her field and the chef in our family, blinks a few times before accepting the steaming cup of Starbucks from my hand. Her hair falls loosely around her face, with random pieces sticking up from sleeping on the chair.

"Thank you." She fixes her hair before taking a long pull from the cup. "Where's Chase?"

"I dropped him off at school. He's got lacrosse, so we're free until four or five tonight. Before you ask, I notified the school. The security guards are on high alert. He's safe."

"Thank you," she says, sounding more relieved than before.

"How's she holding up?" I ask.

Hadley's still sleeping in the same clothes as yesterday. Slumped in her chair, her head rests on the bed with her hand holding onto Logan for dear life.

"Truthfully, she's a good actress. She's keeping a good front, but she's falling apart."

"That's Hadley, always rising above regardless of how she feels. Any changes?"

"No. He's stable," she says. "They're running a toxicology report, testing his blood for whatever they can. The only thing we know for sure is it was an allergic reaction."

"Will's checking into his movements that night, but the kid lives off pizza. Nothing out of the ordinary."

"They're testing everything regardless." Frankie looks over at Hadley, concern etched all over her face. "Taking her to work?"

"Yeah, no optional delay. Some bullshit about contracts, rentals, and all that. Security's been increased, and I'll be with Hadley until she's done."

"She staying with us?" she asks.

"I'd feel better if she did. Everyone under one roof, ya know?"

"You don't think that's dangerous with Chase in the house?"

"We've got an alarm, a patrol car outside, and a safe with weapons inside; I think we're good."

"I get it, several layers of defense before the guns," she says, rubbing the sleep from her eyes. "Please don't say that in front of Chase. I don't need him searching for them to play *Call of Duty* for real."

"Understood. Go home. Sleep." I pull her into a tight hug and kiss her forehead. "I'm sorry this is our honeymoon."

"It's the life we've chosen, Jasmine." Her lips grace mine before she pushes away and smiles sleepily. She grabs her things and kisses Hadley on the head before walking out the door.

"Hadley." I gently touch her shoulder, trying to wake her up. "Had, you need to get up now." I push a little bit harder.

"I don't want to go."

"I know, Had, but the officers outside will take good care of him. If they need anything or something happens, we'll be back here."

"He could die before we get here." She raises her head, showing her tired and tear-streaked face. "I don't want to leave him alone."

"How about we go over to the set and you talk to your bosses in person? You explain what you want, and then we come back here. Unless you can call them?"

"No, face to face is best. A drive won't hurt, but they'll call if something happens?"

"It's the law, Hadley. They will call you for medical decisions."

She stumbles as she tries to stand up. I quickly wrap my arms around her and pull her into a tight embrace. She takes several shallow breaths, her left hand continuing to hold Logan's right. I feel the struggle within her as she releases his hand to flop lifelessly to the bed.

"Let's get this over with."

Keeping my right arm around her, I lead her out of the room. The two uniformed officers nod at me before closing the door behind us. The captain put a high-level security protocol in place. No one sees Logan without the proper identification and if they're not on the list of approved individuals. It's a difficult and overly annoying process, but I'm thankful he put it in play.

"Did you park in the garage?" Her voice comes out as a small whisper.

"No, I parked in the private garage below the hospital."

"How'd you manage that?"

"You're Hadley Moreno. You're the new up-and-coming "it" girl, and they'd rather let me park in some CEO's spot than have a scandal outside their door."

"You flashed your badge, didn't you?"

"I plead the fifth." I shrug.

The elevator dings and the doors shudder open. Leading Hadley inside, I push the *G4* button and wait for the doors to close. She leans into me, her head pressed into my shoulder as her arms tighten around me.

"I won't let anyone see you. Promise."

"They find a way. You know that."

"Not this time."

The elevator shakes as it slows to a stop and Hadley pulls impossibly closer to me. Her face turns toward me to shield her from the invasion of the outside world. The doors rumble as they open to absolute silence. Stretching out my left arm, I place it against the doors, preventing them from closing again.

Hadley's grip loosens a bit, and I feel her head turn to the opening. Within seconds, her muscles relax, and she extracts herself from the safety of my body. The two of us exit the elevator and walk into an abandoned level of the parking garage. My SUV with illegal tint sits a few feet in front of us.

"There's no one here."

"I told you. Now let's get you to the studio before your bosses send out the search party."

"You flashed your badge." A smile barely breaks the empty look she's worn since last night.

"This level is only used for the corporate paper pushers who make hospitals a ton of money. I meant what I said before: showing a somber Hadley Moreno would not be a smart view for their bottom line. Everything would be under a microscope."

"Especially if he dies." The words wash over the two of us like a cold breeze off the Hudson River in winter.

"Yeah, but they won't let that happen."

I open the back door of my SUV and motion for Hadley to get in. "I know it's uncomfortable, but if you lie down, the leeches out front won't see you. They'll barely make you out normally with my tint, but I don't want to take any chances."

She curls up into a ball on the back seat in silence. Closing the door behind her, I run around to the driver's side and get the car moving.

As I ascend ramp after ramp, more and more people mill about. Some are photographers, others just going about their normal business. At the main entrance, the police direct traffic through the swelling crowd. Fans with cell phones in the air record everything while the true paparazzi wait for a glimpse—news media vans with raised antennas air shooting updates as I turn down the street. No one follows me or is aware of the cargo I carry.

***

The ride from Bellevue to Chelsea Piers is as smooth as humanly possible. Hadley sits up when we are a few blocks away from the hospital but keeps her focus outside the window. Pulling up to the side entrance, a security detail waves at my vehicle as if I were a fan trying to break my way in.

"You need to turn around," the guard screams at me. Hadley lowers the window in the back, and the man immediately changes tactics. "I'm sorry, Ms. Moreno. You can drive in there and park." He waves his hands around as if I know where he's referring to.

"Drive inside the building, Jazz. Security will take your keys and move your car to the secure lot," she mumbles from the back.

"I thought we were leaving right after you talk to them."

"They still have to move your car. Like it or not, someone is going to change your seat settings. Just get on with it."

"Dammit. It takes forever to get it just right," I fire back, trying to keep the humor alive in the car. Hadley leans back, and the conversation dies as quickly as it began.

Random people with earpieces wave me around the building and into a massive opening. Hadley hops out of the car before I turn it off and walks inside as if she owns the place. A guard walks up to me as I stumble to get out of the driver's side and catch up.

"Ma'am, keys."

"Ignition," I barely get out as I run into the building.

Walking inside is like walking into Times Square full of tourists stopping to take photos as residents push through to get to work. People rush all over the place, racks of clothing flying by as I try to navigate the entryway. Seeing a glimpse of Hadley's hair swinging back and forth, I rush in that direction, giving apologies as I bump into someone every other footfall.

"Dammit, Hadley, you can't run off." I spin the woman around, and she is most decidedly not my Hadley. "Sorry, I thought you were Hadley Moreno."

"I don't know who you are, but Ms. Moreno doesn't do interviews or speak to fans while at work," she says.

"I'm not—"

"I don't care. Security!" Three burly men that make my tall frame look minuscule surround us before I can state my case. "This person has no credentials to be on set," she says before storming off in a different direction.

"Guys, if you'll just give me a second to explain."

"If you'd please follow us to the exit," one of them says and stands directly in front of me.

"If you would just find Hadley, she'll explain why I'm here."

"Right, and you know Mr. Jackman as well."

"Jackman . . . as in Hugh Jackman? He's here? Holy shit." The guy in front of me takes two steps forward, forcing me backward toward the exit. "No, seriously, I am here in a professional capacity for Hadley Moreno. I'm a detective in the NYPD."

"Okay, that's it." I'm spun around and lifted off the ground by one of the men. My head hits his lower back as he flings me over his shoulder like I weigh nothing.

"Wait!" I hear someone yell in the background. The guards stop walking as a woman in all black walks up to the men and speaks in hushed tones. I'm lowered back to a standing position before the three men disperse without an apology. The middle-aged woman shoves a plastic card into my hand while I try to calm the pure embarrassment of being carried like a child.

"You have to wear this somewhere visible at all times. Never speak to anyone or acknowledge the cast when you pass by. You are here as a visitor and support for Ms. Moreno. And no video or audio recording. Do you understand?"

"I guess."

"Good, this way."

Walking past a door that reads Carpentry, the sound of table saws and nail guns overpower the voices nearby. I turn down a long hallway and follow my surly host. I pass several doors with no markings on them. People exit and enter, but their purpose is completely unknown to me.

My cop instincts begin to go into overdrive.

There are so many rooms, so many places to hide and ways to get in. I doubt if security and these credentials are enough to stop anyone from having access.

"Can you tell me how secure this place is?" I ask. She continues to ignore me, and we walk up a flight of stairs to an area labeled Mezzanine—an exact copy of the floor below with a myriad of unmarked doors.

"In here, please." She stands holding open a door for me. Entering the room, I see there's a small table with some chairs around it; no information about the situation, and worse: no Hadley.

"I need to see Ms. Moreno."

"You'll see her shortly. Someone will be here in a moment," she says before turning and briskly closing the door, locking me in here alone. I look over my cell phone for any calls or texts I may have missed while I was in this mess outside. The door swings open, and two young men walk in wearing jeans and sport jackets. They look like cookie-cutter copies of one another except for the facial hair on the male to my right.

"Please, sit."

"No, thanks. Where is Ms. Moreno."

"Ignore my brother. I'm Jake, and this is John. We're working with the producers to ensure this project goes off without a hitch."

"Nice to meet you J squared, but where is Hadley Moreno?"

"Ms. Moreno is currently in makeup, getting ready for her scenes today. She's explained the situation, and we are truly sorry for everything that's gone on."

"If you're sorry, why is she in makeup and not heading back to the hospital?"

"I'm sure you understand there's a lot that goes into making a film of this magnitude. I won't bore you with the details, but to stop this production would cost the studio a lot of money. Ms. Moreno has agreed to continue filming with the stipulation that you and your team have access as well as emergency leave if the hospital rings," Jake says. He runs a hand through his salt-and-pepper hair before sitting down and crossing his legs. John drops a small folder on the table in front of him before following his doppelganger in finding a chair.

"Great, so where do I go . . ."

"I wish you could do that, but right now we need to handle your clearance."

John pushes the file across the table. I flip it open; there are twenty or thirty pages of paper in there. "You'll find it's a standard nondisclosure agreement. Each member of your team will fill one out before their first shift. They will be provided a visitor card when they arrive, which must be returned upon exiting the facility."

"So, you want me to kill a tree so no one can find out that Hadley is starring in a Hugh Jackman film?"

"Precisely. You cannot speak of this to anyone, post anything on social media, or even allude to the shoot at any given time."

"Okay. One: I don't have social media. Two: I don't give a shit about your film shoot. I want to keep my friend safe from any harm that might befall her. So, you can take the paperwork and shove it."

"You sign or we will have you removed from this location," Jake says behind his ever-annoying early-nineties-styled stubble.

"Fine. Then am I allowed to see Ms. Moreno?"

"I believe Hillary informed you of the rules?"

"Is that the happy robot who brought me here?" I say and roll my eyes. "Yeah, I got it. Don't touch anything. I'm not to be seen nor heard; basically act like a five-year-old at an adult's party?"

"I'm glad we understand one another. You can skip to the signature pages unless you wish to read it all."

Looking over the pile, I go against my better judgment and flip to the signature pages. Once that's done, the twin misfits walk me out of the room and across the hall. Hadley rests on a couch wearing a full-body leather outfit.

"What happened to heading back to the hospital?" I ask softly as the door shuts behind me.

"Powers that be changed my mind," she answers.

"We can walk if you want. Nothing is stopping us."

"My contract is." Hadley spins around and thuds her leather boots on the floor. "We have a specific deadline, and if I force a delay or walk, they can sue me for the entire budget. Not to mention it could destroy my reputation and career."

"Hadley, Logan—"

"Is not my husband or my biological family." She spits out. "At least that's what my agent says."

Before I can reply, there's a knock at the door, and the Hadley look-alike enters in the same full-body outfit. I lean against the wall behind the door and say nothing.

"Hey, you okay? You look like shit."

"Thanks, Megan. Really."

"I heard about Logan. I hope he's okay."

"I'll know more soon. Did you work on the new stunt? Anything I should know?" Hadley tries to move the topic to something more comfortable.

"No, we're all good. By the way, did security tell you about this freak who was screaming downstairs? She was all "I need to see Hadley Moreno" and how she's going to protect you. I had security throw her out. When will those people realize they can't just walk onto the set as they please?"

"You had security throw her out?" Hadley says with a genuine smile on her face, the first one I've seen in a few days.

"Yeah, we have to stick together."

Hadley points behind Megan as she continues to hold her half-smirk. The woman turns around and stops when her eyes meet mine. I can't tell if she's confused, angry, or out of her element. Her face is expressionless, as if she had too many shots of Botox.

"Megan, this is my best friend, Jasmine Steele. She's a detective in the NYPD."

"It's nice to meet you, Megan." I hold my hand out for her. Her eyes lower to my hand and then back up to my face.

"Germaphobe, you understand," she says offhandedly before turning her attention back to Hadley. "I didn't know you knew her. I was looking out for your best interest."

"It's fine," Hadley says. "I just need a minute with Jazz, and I'll be right down, okay?"

Megan takes her cue and almost runs out of the room. "Those people?" I ask.

"She's a damn good stunt double, and she is a nice person when you get to know her. I swear she's not normally like that."

"Might not be, but damn she sucks at first impressions."

"Like someone else I know." Hadley raises her eyes at me. "Any updates?"

"No. The team is sorting through all your fan mail, and we'll go from there. Anything from the docs?"

"No. That's a good thing, right?" she asks.

"Yeah, I assume so."

"I gave the hospital the main office line here since I can't have my cell phone downstairs. You ought to turn yours off."

"I already put it on silent."

"Doesn't matter. The call might interfere with the wireless equipment. Please, text everyone before turning it off." Hadley stands and pats herself down. "You ready for this?"

"I'll send a quick text to Will explaining the situation. Are you? Ready for this, that is?"

"Sweetheart, I was made for this shit." Her confidence comes back in waves as we walk through the doorway and back down to the main floor.

Following Hadley like a puppy dog, I watch how she commands the room: shoulders pulled back, confident steps as people throw things in front of her and fire off questions. She's in her element, and it shows. Walking into a giant area labeled Studio D, I stand off to the side as far as possible while still keeping Hadley in my view. With cameras all about, crew members set everything up for the shot, and I am so proud of my friend.

Right now, at this moment, she is shining above all the darkness. All those haters who told her she was all tits and no brains. All the tweets, reviews, Facebook hate mail—all of it is thrown out the window as she stands next to the leading man. She's accomplished her dreams and succeeded where everyone said she would fail. I couldn't be prouder.

No one will take this away from her. Not while her chosen family is protecting her. They'll find themselves in a small cell before that happens. I promise.

Chapter Five

After a full twelve hours on set, which I was assured was a short day, Hadley wanted to get to the hospital. I manage to get about six hours of shuteye in the most uncomfortable chair imaginable. I wonder if they do this deliberately. Maybe they make the visitors not want to stay for too long so they can work. It felt that way when I was visiting my oma in rehab for a hip replacement. I would stay as long as I could during visiting hours, just to be bumped, shushed, or downright disregarded when the staff would come in. She healed poorly, and when the second hip failed, there was no rehab. There was her house, her pup, and her family. Doctors were impressed with her recovery then.

Will came by and forced me out around eight in the morning with an herbal tea from my favorite Starbucks and a message from the captain. That's why I am sitting in our basement office with no one around but me. The new whiteboard is empty, desks deserted, and the coffee maker is cold. The silence is deafening, the emptiness unnerving as the newness has yet to pass fully.

"Steele, glad you're here." The voice of Agent Karina Marlow rings out from the elevator before the doors close.

"Cap said to check in, but I think everyone else missed the memo."

"No, they're on assigned duties," she answers curtly. The last time we were around one another, she was firm and fierce but also had this glow around her. Her family always kept her head above the darkness. The woman in front of me now looks tired and worn. Her eyes are less vibrant, and her shoulders hunch slightly forward as if she's lost her strength to stand upright.

"It's been a long time, Karina. I'm glad you're here working with us again. Is this a permanent change, or are you the FBI liaison of the month?"

"Since Will has only been cleared recently for full active duty, he will be taking care of Hadley's transportation to and from work. He will also be ensuring her safety to your home. I understand she feels safer there, but if the location is disclosed to the public, we will have to change it. Did you give him your badge for clearance?"

"Yes." I take a small break to take in her all-business side. "Karina, what's going on? Is this about your ex-husband Simon? I called, but you never—"

"Detective Locke is working with Mr. Pevy's second to run the tech department. She seems to be handling herself quite well down there," Karina continues, ignoring my question.

"I know. Apparently she's a computer science nerd. You going to answer my question or continue to be on edge without giving me any insight here?"

"Doctor Hayes is handling the victims of a few other cases, so unless there is a body, he will not be needed nor pulled away from his duties."

"I figured." My voice is flat and emotionless as I let her go through her details. Her body movements are sharp and jagged. It's as if she's conflicted with no real outlet for any of that energy. I know she's been through hell over the last year, but I don't want to force her to talk.

"Doctor Brown is still processing the evidence that the crime scene unit lifted from both apartments. It will take some time, but they have been cleared to use overtime as needed."

"How did you pull that one off?" I ask.

"I made a phone call and a proper request," she answers coldly. "If you logged into the police portal, you would find all the necessary files to expedite any and all requests."

"And you would find it still sits on the desk of the powers that be until the old goats have their secretaries print it out for them. Then it sits there until you no longer need their help." I laugh at the idiocy of the streamlined service. The more technology advances to help us out, the more people rail against it.

"We want to ensure we follow the rules, dot our i's and cross our t's. I'd rather not lose a case or screw up because we missed something or signed the paper in the wrong damn place," Karina counters quickly.

"Where's Captain Zeile? I've tried to reach out to him, but he hasn't been in his office."

"Meeting with my boss, among others, as he explains the need for this team and the . . . unorthodox means of handling these cases."

"Karina, you've worked with us before. You know how we do things. Sometimes we might bend a rule or two, but it's never to the detriment of the case."

"Maybe not, or maybe you got lucky, Jasmine. If you follow the book, maybe you wouldn't miss what might be right under your nose," she says louder than needed. "Maybe things would be done properly and the paperwork filed on time and not sitting on your desk. Maybe victims would have the justice they so desperately need in a timely fashion. Hell, maybe the justice system would move faster!" She's nearly yelling at the end. I wonder if this is directed at me or her ex-husband. As her friend, I'm an easy target, one who will take the beating and forgive her.

"If we all lived in 'maybes' or 'what-ifs,'" I say, "we'd never get anything done. We would point fingers and blame one another for everything."

I rub the back of my neck as it has continued to tighten up throughout this conversation. "I don't know what's going on with you, Karina, but this doesn't sound like you. We've been in touch since you left New York. Hell, I gave Sydney your number for help on a case. I've come to think we're friends, Karina. I've also seen the headlines and heard the rumors. I can't imagine how you feel, but I'm here for you when you're ready to talk. I've always been here, okay?" I pause and try to ease my desire to force her to talk. "When you're ready, I'll be here. Until then, can you please talk to me like I'm a normal human being and not some ignorant lackey?"

Karina watches me for a few moments. Her eyes focus firmly on her hands gripped tightly on a file folder. One thumbnail is broken into the meat, jagged and sore. The rest of her nails are perfectly kept.

"I know you mean well, but right now"—she pauses, her fingers going white with the pressure on the file—"I just can't. I need to focus on this right now. I need to assist in getting this department's success rates and your abilities to the forefront of the conversation. I need . . ." Her voice cracks ever so slightly, and she shuts her mouth to prevent more from coming out.

"What do you need from me?" I ask, trying to bring her focus back to something more tangible. Her eyes meet mine and shine with a silent thank-you. Her hands loosen their death grip and drop the file onto my desk. A few pages slide out from the haphazard way it lands. The face of a middle-aged man brightly smiling is the first thing that catches my eye. As I open the folder, several more pictures come into focus. Most are men, as the psychological profile would suggest in this case.

"What am I looking at?"

"Yesterday, the team isolated these individuals as persons of interest." She pauses, her hands wringing together tightly, rubbing against the dry skin. "Do you ever think you're just a cog in this fucked-up machine called justice?"

The change in direction throws me for a second. "All the time," I say. "I'm not one bit special, just another grunt doing what they think is best. The system doesn't belong to me or owe me anything. It'll still be turning long after I'm retired or dead."

"Yet, you run into situations with no concern for those around you? Some careers might have been derailed because of that ask questions later attitude. How do you do it? How do you handle the personal grudges challenging you every step of the investigation?"

"Shit, Karina. That's some heavy questioning there," I say, giving myself some time to think. I don't quite understand her reasoning behind these questions. Her tone is neutral, but I feel attacked by her words. It's been obvious since I got here; Karina is not herself. This is another nail in that coffin. She would normally never ask me things like this.

I answer as honestly as I can. "I had nothing to live for. It's easy to throw yourself into a dangerous situation when your mind is full of dark thoughts."

"You have Chase, Frankie . . . your friends . . ."

"I understand that now, and they are the reason I am more cautious. It's a daily process, but the voices never stop, Karina. You learn to tune them out."

"Shitstorms seem to follow you. Between Irving Garrison's kid killing your brother and his wife while Chase slept in his baby seat to Hadley being targeted now . . . don't you ever wonder which person you love would be next? Did you call or text Hadley and see if she and Logan were okay? Do you obsess about it or do the opposite and never check-in?"

"Okay, this is getting too close for comfort here, and I—"

"I need to know. Please," she says. Her voice is broken; her eyes look for comfort in anything I can add to the conversation.

"You know what we do," I say. "Danger follows everyone, like death. It's always there, lingering in the background, waiting for the right time to strike. You either feed into it and be fearful all the time, or you do the best you can with every breath you take." I try to keep my anxiety in check as the conversation brings up darker memories. I wish I could let go of it—all of it. "Logan had come to me with his concerns, but without proof or Hadley's official complaint, it was out of my hands. We were buried under the Carnation Killer case, and truthfully, I wasn't focused on her newfound fame. Was it wrong? I don't know. But I had a job to do, and at that moment, I did the best I could."

"Hadley would never come to you, would she? Her insecurities and fears of talking to you about it, adding to your stress . . . maybe she was concerned you would go off on your own and try to solve it. Maybe she was afraid you wouldn't take her seriously. This other case took precedence, but did you check on her? Make sure she was okay? You talk about being there for your friends, having their backs, but you let her down. You're a fraud."

Her harsh, clipped words rise in decibel with each line, little knives piercing me as my failures are thrown in my face. My anxiety is fully out of control, my hands shaking, my jaw clenched, and the feeling of fight or flight pushing against my chest.

Her FBI training is on full display now. Her words cut into my weaknesses while her stance is one of control. If this were a true interrogation, I would cave in a few minutes. Not because I'm a pathetic soul, but because Karina is so damned good at her job.

In that instance, I couldn't leave. Right now, though, I can run far away and cut her off. I could walk away, be professional and cold until she transferred. I could destroy the friendship that we've built. The old me would choose that easily—the simpler option. I'm trying to be better, and facing the fight ripping me apart inside is part of the process.

"I never claimed to be perfect." The words eke out through gritted teeth. "I'm human, and I am seriously flawed, but I've never denied a friend help when they asked for it. I gave up an entire year of my life to take care of someone I cared about. I gave up my life for them . . . and I was tossed away like trash once they didn't need me anymore. We're all broken, Karina. I just accept it better than you do."

Her face changes. Maybe she sees the damage her words have done, but she remains silent. I grab my car keys, not trusting myself to speak any further. Logically, I understand her negative emotions are not directed at me, but my feelings have been hurt nonetheless. I'd rather get out of the situation than make it worse.

The friend I've enjoyed playing video games with, texting whenever we were free, and talking out details of a case is hidden behind a wall of pain. I can't crack it, nor can I force her to let me in. Thankfully, the elevator announces its presence so I won't have to continue fighting my inner thoughts.

An officer exits and holds some papers out for Karina. Her eyes break off our staring contest, allowing me to slip into the box and to another level away from the tension. The words though . . . they remain deeply seated in my box of vulnerabilities.

***

Sydney sitting behind Logan's desk looks wrong and out of place. She shows no signs of slowing down though as her fingers move a mile a minute over the keyboard. A low bass beat pumps out of her headphones as she dances to it. After a few minutes, she looks up and catches my half-hearted wave. She turns off the music and sits back in her chair.

"Anything?" I ask.

"Managed to scour all the emails pretty quickly with a program. Sent a list to Agent Marlow to process. The social media accounts are harder, though: tons of fake profiles, tons of people screaming vulgarities with the idiotic idea of free speech. Hell, a young kid who swears he's over thirteen called her a slut that he would ram into oblivion. That was the polite phrasing. His other posts are somewhat grotesque in their violent phrasing. He also corresponds with a lot of repeat offenders. He seems to be the most active on all her social media accounts."

"Enough to look into?"

"Considering the deluge of his comments and posts about her . . . .possibly."

"He live around here?" I ask, and Sydney's fingers race across the keyboard with efficiency.

"Thomas Catz, sixteen, lives in Sticksville. Why?"

"Print it all out."

"Steele, he's in school right now."

"Good. Where?"

"Catholic School out east."

"Perfect little Catholic boy isn't he?" I say as I glance at my watch. "By the time we get there, he should be home barring any after-school activities."

"Steele, maybe this isn't a good idea. You seem to be on edge about something."

"Yup, a lot of things. It doesn't stop the fact that you have a young kid threatening Hadley before her boyfriend was attacked. He might not have done anything, but considering his activities, maybe he knows more than his tweets reflect."

"Okay," Sydney says before hitting a few keys. "I'll keep the team searching through video footage outside Logan's apartment."

"I thought his building didn't have any."

"They don't, but there's a bank on one corner and a luxury high-rise on the other. We're slowly scouring it to confirm the delivery of the pizza. Maybe we can figure out who delivered."

"Forgive me if I'm stepping on toes here, but why not just call the pizza place and ask who delivered it?"

"They swear that Logan ordered delivery but sent someone to pick it up for him instead."

"Video inside?"

"None. They said it happened sometimes. Logan would pay for delivery, but Will would pick it up on occasion, or even Hadley. Quite the event whenever she went in. Said this guy was new but they didn't think much of it at the time."

"Who the hell knows when someone calls in a pie?"

"He calls in the same order every week like clockwork."

"Same day every week?"

"According to the pizza shop, Will and Hadley . . . yeah."

"Gamer friends?"

"Will contacted them and got their statements." Sydney digs through some paperwork on Logan's desk before finding a sheet with notes all over it. "Logan was active and playing from about nine at night. Rebecca mentioned he was coughing a lot but that he told them all his allergies were out of control. Akuni and Charlie corroborate the story."

"Okay, but when we found him, he wasn't logged into any game. Probably pushed back to the main menu with inactivity. Did his friends mention when he ducked out?"

"No, they couldn't remember an exact time. Akuni said he noticed Logan missing around midnight."

"How can you *not* notice someone not talking in the chat or helping out on a mission? That's a bit out there."

"According to Charlie, they were in a large group mission with over twenty people on a team. He tried to have a private chat, but there were network errors. He kept calling it a *Ubi-Glitch*. Something to do with the manufacturer."

"My brain is overloading with this gaming talk. What's the bottom line?"

"Logan ordered his personal pizza like he did every week for game night. Someone picked it up, delivered it, and he went into anaphylaxis sometime while his team was looting for new weapons."

"Remind me to take away Chase's Xbox."

"You have one too."

"I'm an adult."

"So were Logan and his friends. This isn't a gaming issue, it's a—"

"I know, it's an asshole issue." I rub my eyes and feel the exhaustion forming behind them. "Let's go check this kid out. See if he knows something. If nothing else, maybe we wake him up to the fact that social media posts are forever."

"Does Chase have any accounts?" Sydney questions while packing things up.

"No way in hell," I answer confidently.

"Ahh, so none that you're aware of," she says as she passes me quickly.

"What do you mean aware of? He can't set them up without an adult, right?" I plead with Sydney as we hop in the elevator to the garage.

"Technically, no, but if he has your information, he can easily set it up. Plus, all you need to do is put in a birthday that makes you a minimum of thirteen. Then you roll back the year until your age catches up. Not like the big companies care; it's a numbers game paid in people and rubles for election time." She smiles and laughs before stopping short. "Should we let Agent Marlow know where we're going?"

"Send her a text when we're on the island away from the city."

"She'll be pissed."

"Nothing we can do right now. Doc Brown is still working on the evidence. The techs are scouring all the digital shit they can, and Hadley is being protected. The sad fucking state of a stalking case: we have to wait for him to strike again."

"Isn't that every case?"

"Now you're getting the job, Sydney."

Hopefully, this kid gives us some clue to go on. The idea of driving out to Nassau County isn't a thrilling one, especially since we'll hit traffic on the way back. Karina will be stewing by the time we return. I expect her to be in full screaming mode about wasting time on a fool's errand. Right now, though, it's all I can do with what we've got. When I get back, maybe she'll let me handle speaking to those case files. Until then, I guess I'll do the best I can and pray for something positive.

Chapter Six

Sticksville, a town I haven't returned to since I left years ago. It's a beautiful cornucopia of diversity that taught me more about myself than anything else. It's also a town with a dark underbelly, one that harbors resentment, conspiracy theories, and a hidden anger. The other, lovelier, residents just smiled all the time, and showed compassion to their fellow neighbor. I loved it here until the McMansions started popping up all over. I missed having a place to park and quiet in my yard.

My childhood home, bought for a small sum when my parents were first married, was now being estimated at a million-dollar-plus sale. Frankie and I had moved into a small studio apartment when my mother passed away. I told Henry that he and Belinda should move into our childhood home with Chase, but he didn't feel it was appropriate. He sold it and said he would handle the money, including my cut. Even to this day, finances are not my forte, so Frankie handles it all.

Whatever Henry did paid off greatly. When he and Belinda were murdered, Chase had a college fund, and I had more than enough to put a sizeable down payment on a place in Brooklyn during a police auction. Sure, the fact that a drug cartel ran a criminal enterprise through the place might have turned away a lot of customers. It didn't help that the walls and floors were destroyed when the search warrant came through. That all worked to our advantage. When it burned down, we rebuilt thanks to insurance, friends, and increasing our mortgage a bit with refinancing. Ironically, I love my little postage stamp area, small driveway for one car, and minuscule privacy considering what I left behind.

"We're here." The words come out of my mouth and echo across the truck. "Cookie-cutter McMansion, double car driveway, basketball hoop in the backyard, and a well-maintained front yard."

"Meaning?" Sydney leads.

"It means they take care of their house, or they prefer to keep up appearances." I open the door and wait for Sydney before walking to the front entrance. The door opens a few seconds after the doorbell rings.

A tall and slender young woman answers. "Can I help you?" Her curls bounce off her shoulders as her smile reveals full braces.

"Hi, my name is Detective Steele, and this is Detective Locke with the NYPD. Is your mother home?" The young girl stares at our badges, verifying them as much as a teenager can.

"Mom!" she screams before closing the door in our faces. Sydney stifles a laugh as the door opens once again, revealing an older woman, obviously well-kept: jeans, button-down shirt, fuzzy slippers, and a Bluetooth device in her ear.

"Janet, you've made great progress thus far. Why don't we hold these thoughts until next week?" Her higher-than-anticipated voice cuts my eardrums in half as it radiates down the block. "Don't worry about Dylan or anything else this week. I want you to focus on your healing and not sex. It's not always about intercourse, but the journey leading up to it."

"Is she having a therapy session with someone while we're standing here?" Sydney whispers to me.

"Unethical, but no legal statutes bind her."

"Common decency isn't a law?"

"Not yet."

"Excuse me, detectives. How can I help you?" she asks.

"Are you Mrs. Catz?" I ask.

"It's Ms." She stands, hand on her hip, seemingly annoyed at us for having a conversation with one another.

"We were hoping we could speak to your son Thomas," Sydney answers quickly.

"In regard to?" She folds her arms across her chest as her eyes dart back and forth between us.

"I think it would be best if we speak inside, ma'am."

"I don't legally have to let you in. So, unless you wish to share what this is about, you have a good day." The woman steps to the side, her intention clear.

Sydney pulls out a printout from Thomas's Twitter page and hands it to his mother. I have no idea which one she presented, but Ms. Catz's look of sheer embarrassment tells me everything I need to know.

"Well, I mean . . . boys will be boys," she says, handing the page back to Sydney.

"Yes, ma'am, they will be," Sydney says. "However, credible threats have come forward, and we need to speak to everyone we can—"

"Are you saying my sixteen-year-old son hurt this woman? He's been home all week by nine. Nothing more to discuss."

"We don't believe he was directly involved in anything, ma'am. We need to discuss a forum he actively participates in. You can stay with us the entire time, but I assure you we only want to get some information. Nothing more."

"This is ridiculous. I won't allow it."

"She's right," I say to Sydney. "This is ridiculous. And it's only social media, right? I'm sure she wouldn't mind us sharing that page you showed her on, I don't know, maybe her Facebook page. I'm sure her patients would be *fascinated* by her little 'boys will be boys' son. Let's go."

I turn to leave and take a step.

"Wait." She senses I'm not bluffing. I stop and turn back. "Okay, but if you step one foot out of line, this conversation is over," she says and steps to the side, allowing us in.

"Thomas, get your hiney down here!" Ms. Catz wails up the stairs before leading us into the living room. "You two sit on the couch, please."

A sullen teenager walks into the living room; his attention is firmly focused on his cell phone as he frantically types away. His baggy baseball shirt hides his slender, yet toned, frame. He falls into a seat across from the couch, but he has yet to look up.

"Thomas, these people are here to see you."

"One minute, I have to reply to this dude." His thumbs keep moving at the speed of text.

"Mr. Catz, if that could wait—" Sydney tries.

He rudely cuts her off. "It can't." His mother reaches for his phone, but Thomas quickly moves. She contorts her face in anger, but I can't tell if it's at her son or how he is making her look.

"Do you remember telling a Hadley Moreno that you would"—I grab one of the pages from Sydney—"fuck her so hard that her implants would fly out her mouth?"

He stops typing on his phone and finally looks up at the two of us. His mother leans back in her chair with her hand over her eyes.

"Where'd you get that?"

"It's on your Twitter account."

"You can't use that! What's this, government spying on me and shit?" He raises his voice, and it cracks.

"Your profile is public, Mr. Catz," Sydney says simply. "All we did was read your posts and follow the links that you gave freely to the viewing public."

He looks back at his phone and then back to the two of us. His body language is off, as if he wants to fight back but is unsure how to do so.

"Would you like us to continue reading your posts from the last few years? Maybe we should show your mom some videos you favorited?"

"No!" He tries to grab the folder out of Sydney's hands, but she holds firm. It's rather comical how he flails his body around to try and get the file out of her hands. After a few seconds, she releases the file, and he falls backward into the chair.

"You realize it's still available for everyone to see."

"I have a right to make my profiles private. You have no right to come at me like this. I know the law." He jerks his body as he tries to get comfortable in the chair. He looks through the file briefly, his eyes widening at how much we've printed.

"You do have the right to make your profiles private. You also have the right to post as you please," Sydney continues. "But we have the right to compile a digital file for our case. We also have the right to access what you've posted due to the graphic nature of said posts that may or may not have been viable threats against another human being."

"But you—"

"The internet is forever, Mr. Catz. While we're not specifically here for your vulgar posts, the comments of encouragement for putting women in their place, or pornographic video views and likes. We'll leave all that to your parents. We need to discuss the communications between you and other profiles."

"I don't know shit about anybody personally." He looks around the room, trying to deflect the conversation.

"Enough with the language!" his mother says harshly as if she hadn't heard us read his curse-filled rants.

"Mr. Catz, we both know you're lying."

"My son doesn't lie, detective! If he says it was just a stupid site, then it is."

"Ms. Catz, your son likes rape porn videos and discusses defiling women with a voracious appetite. Considering you are unaware of this, I don't believe lying is out of the realm of possibility here," I say, sounding more like Frankie than an actual detective. "Even if you haven't met them in the real world, you have spoken to them before."

"I talk to them. So what?"

"What do you discuss?" Sydney asks while typing notes on her phone. "Do you just reply to each other's posts, direct message, or are you in a group chat together?"

Right away, I am thankful for Sydney's involvement. The more these cases move into the online realm of connections, the more I need insight. I'm not out of touch or too old to follow it, but when you have no patience or time, you invest it differently.

"I mean, yeah," he stammers and shifts uncomfortably.

"Thomas, answer their question correctly," his mother chimes in, again more out of concern for her image than his.

"All of the above."

"What do you talk about in the group chats?" Sydney continues, ignoring his discomfort.

"Stuff."

"Okay, kid, we're trying to make this easier on you and your family. If you don't want to answer, we can arrest you for the threats to Ms. Moreno's person. We'll have our tech team scour your videos to ensure there are no underage individuals in them. If there are, you can be arrested for disseminating child pornography."

"You said—"

"While your mother is correct in her assumption that we are not here to take you in at the moment, your deliberate attempts to impede this investigation can be extrapolated as a crime for hindering prosecution."

"Extrapo what? You can't do that. Mom?"

"Thomas, we're trying to get information that would clear you of the situation we're investigating," Sydney says. "You're evasive for some reason. Tell us what's happening, and maybe we can help. Otherwise, you are forcing us to take you in." Sydney says all this in a calm demeanor the kid might understand.

"We umm . . . we talk about her and some other women," he begins shyly.

"Other women?" Ms. Catz asks incredulously.

"Ms. Catz, if you could please refrain from interjecting, that would be great," I say.

The more she opens her mouth and moves around, I realize she doesn't care about her son. She cares about how she looks in front of us. If this hits the press, it could be bad for her image, and heaven forbid that happens. It's the day and age of instant breaking news that never fades. She would forever be connected to her son and his sexual deviancy and criminal behavior. Instead of worrying about his well-being and getting him help, she's probably thinking about having to hire a publicist to fix her reputation.

"Umm . . . I always think it's stupid, ya know? Like a place to bullshit, try to one-up each other but never actually do it."

"You realize there is another person on the end of those accounts you message, right?" Sydney questions.

"Yeah, but like, celebrities have people to handle all that. I mean, it's not like they're really on their social media pages. And the rest of them, they have low followers, so I don't think they're even reading the comments anyway. Why would our jokes bother them?"

"Because they're people, Thomas. Regardless of their status, they are human beings trying to connect with those who keep them working." I rub my temples. This kid is as clueless as his mother.

"The other women you posted to probably signed off because of comments like yours. Those are harassing and violate the terms and conditions of all social media platforms," Sydney adds.

"I never got banned or warned, so it wasn't wrong," Thomas answers quickly.

"Or they just blocked you and never reported it. Sometimes that's easier than fighting with a company to have explicit content removed," Sydney counters as her calm demeanor washes away.

"Look, just tell us where you got the videos."

"In the group chat. The other guys share links and told me to share them privately on my channel."

"Can you give us the usernames in the chat as well as the link?" I quickly toss out.

"I know I don't have to give you the names, but I'll give you the link." I hand him my old-school notepad, and he writes down a long website address. Sydney hands him a list with a few names on it.

"I understand you don't wish to divulge your associates, but are any of these names familiar?"

"Yeah . . ." Thomas scans the list for a few more moments. "Six of the names, that's it."

"Okay, which ones?"

"I told you . . ." Ms. Catz clears her throat loudly. Thomas looks to her, her arms folded and a stern expression leaving no room for doubt. He shakes his head and reluctantly points to the names on the sheet.

"Thank you." Sydney stands and packs up her things. "We'll be in touch."

Ms. Catz leads us to the door, but I stop and turn my attention back to her son.

"You can delete everything you want off your profiles, but there's always a backup server somewhere. You might want to be careful about what you post from now on."

Sydney and I open the front door and step outside. Behind us, the door slams hard. Through the oak door, we can hear Ms. Catz screaming at the top of her lungs at Thomas. His voice raises as he tries to defend himself. This is the type of family that made me want to leave this town. They've forgotten the meaning of being kind and worry about perception rather than human interaction.

"Make sure you get all the kid's information to the DA."

"We said—"

"Yeah, we did, but he bullied, stalked, harassed . . . it's out of our hands. We report what we find; lawyers sort the rest out," I say, pressing the unlock button on the key fob. "If we don't report it, we're no better than those that partake in it."

"I know you're right, but he's just a kid," Sydney begins as she looks over at me.

"Juvenile detention is filled with kids just being kids. Crime knows boundaries or limits. He needs to be held accountable if the DA thinks he committed a crime. It's up to them what happens from there. It's how we keep order in the system," I say, getting into the car as the rain begins to fall with a smack against the windshield. "So, we get anything from the names he knew on that list?"

"Among the ones he pointed out are the six people Marlow asked us to look into." Sydney hands me the list filled with the names and their social media tags. Stephanie Chalk, Hank Boner, Liz Gentri, Marty Unger, Ivan Topiz, and Randall Cunning stand out from the rest with a small black dot next to their names.

"The kid didn't notice the markings," I say, turning the key to start the engine. "Smart, making it look like a printer issue."

The windshield wipers squeak across the glass as we sit in traffic on the Long Island Expressway. The showers lighten up for a bit, but the darker storm clouds ahead warn of torrential downpours.

"Change is terrifying," Sydney whispers. "But if you're not willing to try something new, advance yourself, you're going to be left behind. Just like you, Steele. You need to get with the tech stuff or the job will move beyond you."

"I know that. It's why I read as much as I do. Logan would send me all these articles from his subscriptions. Anything to keep me in the loop as much as possible. I'll never have the grasp on it you do, but I promise to try. That's all I've got."

"You're a contrarian, Steele."

"No, just a dumbass. Ask my wife; she'll tell you."

Sydney laughs and turns her attention back to the pages in her folder and her notes on the phone. The kid gave us more information than he's aware of, but I'm not sure if any of it is useful. My cell phone rings, and I see Frankie's face on the screen. Sydney's phone chirps out a text as I hit the answer button on the steering wheel.

"Hey, sweetie, what's up?"

"Oh shit!" Sydney says next to me, her eyes glued to the phone. She looks up at me, her face losing color with every passing second.

"Jasmine . . ." Frankie's voice is low and somber, and fear emanates from the only word she utters.

"Sydney, what's up?" The question bounces around the car. The only sound filling my ears are the wipers and my heartbeat.

"Jasmine, please don't . . . Just talk to me, okay?" Frankie reaches out, trying to calm my nerves.

Sydney turns back to her phone, her hands shaking as she scrolls. Her mouth moves to say something, but she covers it at the last second. Her eyes water as the car behind me honks their horn. I start driving, my anxiety pushing into aggression as I press the pedal down harder and flip on the siren and lights.

"Someone talk. Now." My voice is firm and filled with nervous anger. The scream of my siren filters through the neighborhood. My instinct says to get back to the city now by any means necessary.

"Hadley's been shot," Sydney says.

My instincts were right.

Chapter Seven

"*D octors have informed us that actress Hadley Moreno was brought to the hospital with a gunshot wound to the chest. She was rushed into surgery upon arrival. Police are scouring the area and asking anyone with information about the attack to call their tip line. Just this past week, Ms. Moreno's boyfriend, Logan Pevy, was also hospitalized with an undisclosed illness, but sources tell us he may have been poisoned. The two are here at Bellevue Hospital in a private room under what witnesses are calling a heavy police presence. Authorities are quiet about tying the two cases together, but witnesses have said Detective Jasmine Steele, Ms. Moreno's close friend and the inspiration for her award-winning role in* Ties That Bind, *has been at the crime scene. It's unclear if she will be heading the investigation. Back to you in the studio.*"

Flipping channels brings up another channel covering the attack on Hadley, this time from a paparazzi magazine that thrives on tormenting others for a boost in ratings rather than honest reporting. The unsteady cell phone video shows Hadley in her full leather getup running down the street after another actor. A single shot fires, and the cell phone video violently shakes before the person behind the device hides behind a small wall. I assume they were shooting footage from a rooftop across the street. It's the only explanation for the angle and the distance.

Moving to an alternate channel, a different-angled video shows the aftermath: Hadley, lying on the ground, Will above her barking orders to those around him. Most people remain hidden behind barriers, certainly afraid of more gunfire. Cell phones are out taking pictures, video, or streaming live on social media for the masses to witness. The world would know she was shot before her parents. It's a terrifying prospect but a very real one.

"Steele?" Karina walks in and stands next to me. "They've cleared the area. We've been given permission to investigate the scene."

I turn off the television in the mobile command center, grab my badge and gun, and exit the vehicle.

"Steele, if you can't . . ." she starts. I ignore her attempt at conversation and walk out the door.

People litter the sidewalks. Some are there to see the scene and pay their respects, but I'm sure the majority are there to gain social media notoriety for their fifteen minutes of fame. It gives them a chance to show empathy for someone they will never know but can use to connect to others and bolster their name. The shallow bottom feeders who thrive on grief and torment for likes and retweets. The need to be famous regardless of how or on whose back grates my compassion to a nonexistent level.

I duck under the yellow tape, blink away the residual effects of flashing lights in the darkness, and come slowly up to the scene. My feet stop two steps away from the barricades as an icy chill runs up my spine to the base of my neck, causing me to shiver. The concrete is brand new—white and perfect—but not on three squares. The reddish-brown pool and blood smears pull my gaze to it. I've got a visual of Hadley squirming and screaming as the fluid slowly eases out of her body. I shake my head to clear that thought away. She needs me to focus, not fall apart.

Karina walks past along the edge of my vision. Her head swivels to me and the scene in front of us. My heart pounds harder in my chest as I try to calculate the amount of blood left behind. The news said she's in surgery, but seeing the amount on the ground makes me wonder about her chances of survival.

I pull my eyes away from stains and see the numbered yellow cones which the forensics team has laid out. Various people in police vests continue to photograph and lay out the scene. It's a tornado of activity in a precise and organized manner. It gives me something to focus on as my breathing slows to normal.

"Steele," Captain Zeile says to me, his hand gently resting on my shoulder. "Maybe you should go home. Be with your family right now."

I look beyond him and see Karina talking to a large, muscular man in a security guard's uniform. A pair of handcuffs rest on his belt, but he has nothing else to assist in restraining anyone.

"Steele . . . Jasmine." Zeile squeezes my shoulder tighter. "Go home."

"I can't." I look up at him as my voice wavers slightly. I'm sure my blue eyes are red from the tears that fell during the well-above-speed-limit trip back to the city. "I need to do something, please."

"This is your family, Steele. You shouldn't—"

"Cap, I need to do something. If I go home, I'm going to be useless for the kid and wife. I need to process. Just give me something to do please. I'll be okay."

He continues to stare at me for a few seconds before nodding his head. "Okay, but—"

"How many shots?"

"Witnesses picked up one shot, but others say there were more. Last tally, up to three shots."

"Direction?"

"She was walking north, so the assumption is a southerly direction. We've been looking through footage, but . . ."

"Online clips were vague at best. Once the first shot was fired, they got shaky for obvious reasons."

"We hope that forensics will find more than witnesses for obvious reasons."

"Did ShotSpotter pick up anything on its sensors in this area? The city spent millions on this system to automatically detect the sound of gunshots. Can we use it to triangulate where the shooter was standing? Type of gun? Anything?"

"We were given this location the moment the first shot was fired. After that, officers were dispatched, and an additional shot was picked up. Right now, we're unsure if it was friendly fire or the perp."

"Where's Will? Was he . . .?"

"No, he's fine. He was out of the shot—" Zeile feels me wince under his grasp. "Sorry, poor choice of words. Hadley was in the middle of a scene, cameras rolling, so Will was standing off to the side out of the way. Until further notice, he's her handler and protector agent."

"I'll stop by later tonight. Maybe bring the kid by tomorrow. He's going to want to see Hadley for himself." The random words flow out of my mouth without thought. I feel my body fighting shock, but I need to get to work. I need to remain impartial and be smart—no impropriety when dealing with evidence or searching for it. I have to follow Karina on this one and do everything by the book.

"We've locked the building down tight. No one goes in or out without an escort and only if it's for investigative purposes. Agent Marlow and I are handling the hospital details, access, and security. The press is crowding the front entrance, and they might show up at your house. You know the rules, and until we have a plan in place, you can't visit. I'm sorry."

"Cap, she's one of my best friends. You can't prevent me from seeing her."

"Jesus, look around you, Jasmine. Your face is going to be on the front page of every paper tomorrow, and it's already online. *Hadley Moreno's friend grieves at the scene of the crime.* Everyone from Yonkers to Long Island who doesn't already know you will know what you look like. Anywhere you go, they'll follow. I'll let you handle the mundane parts of this case, but you're going to have to trust Karina and me. No running in guns blazing, remember? We're a team; let us handle it. Once it's clear, you'll be the first number I call."

"You'll keep me posted on any changes, right? Same with Logan?"

"Of course. You have my word."

"Anyone get ahold of their families?"

"It's being handled."

I finally acquiesce. "I don't like it."

"You don't have to, but I'm asking you to follow orders this time. For the sake of everyone involved in this case, please."

"Was already planning on it." The venom in my tone hits the captain in the chest. "Give me something to do, Cap," I say, looking back at Karina and the security guard.

"Agent Marlow, George." Zeile waves the two of them over to us. "I was just telling Detective Steele that you were willing to show her the surveillance from today."

"Sir, I already explained that without a warrant, we won't be releasing the footage."

"We aren't removing it from the property," Karina says. "And we will sign nondisclosure agreements should the footage give too much of the film away. So, there shouldn't be an issue. Once we get the warrant, the team will get copies. Agreed?" Her tone leaves no room for discussion.

"I don't think the NDA will be necessary. Producers lock up that footage." George caves at her words, but he leaves me confused. His closed-circuit camera feed would show the same as the film crew's, so paperwork should be signed. I think under normal circumstances, the guard would have picked up on his mistake, but no one wants a murdered Hollywood actress on their watch. He's showing a slight argument for the audience, nothing more.

George tilts his head in the direction of the studio before walking away. I shove my hands in my pockets as I follow behind him. I hang my head low, hoping to hide from as many cameras as possible. Cap's right, though; the internet sleuths will dig up all those images of Hadley, Frankie, and me from her red-carpet event and plaster it back on the front page. Given my history, everyone is going to expect me to go off the deep end and break protocol. I can't do anything like that; not this time. It's an unnerving idea, putting my full trust in the team around me, but I have no choice. The magnifying glass is focusing and the light on my back burns.

"This way, watch your step," George says over his shoulder as he enters the building and turns down the first hallway.

The place is deserted. Wardrobe racks rest where they were abandoned in the mass exodus. Props litter the floor along with various items of garbage I'm sure were dropped in a flight mentality. I bump a metal sword that falls and hits the wall, and the sound rattles down the hallway.

"I said watch your step!" George almost screams at me.

"Right. Because a prop sword is so much more important than the human being shot outside." The words come out harsh and swift.

"Look, detective, I don't know what you're feeling, but Ms. Moreno has always been very kind to me. Keeping unauthorized people out was a big part of my job. Helping keep people safe . . . I couldn't control what happened, but the rules inside the building I can enforce. So, please, watch your step and allow me to have . . ." His voice breaks as the muscles in his arms flex. I assume George is trying to gain some control over his emotions. We all are.

"Understood."

The security guard turns around in perfect military spin and continues on his way. I step over the sword and around a wardrobe rack to continue following him.

"Did you see it in real time?" I ask.

"No, I was on lunch when it happened."

"Who was working?"

"I honestly don't know. When production switches to outside locations, retired or off-duty officers handle security. The studio hires us, and our jurisdiction ends at the gate."

"Were the cast and crew interviewed by police?"

"I'm not sure. In the event of an emergency, we evacuate all personnel to a secondary location. I know the scene outside included just two actors and minimal crew. The rest were inside, setting up the next sequence. When I was shown the breakdowns for today, we all thought it would be an easy shift. Hell, I told my wife I'd be home for dinner. The first time this month."

George turns the key in a locked door, opening it up to a small, walk-in-closet-sized room. The right wall is lined with small LCD monitors. The only furniture is a desk with a console covered in a shit ton of buttons and two rolling chairs. I walk in and sit in the farthest chair from the door. George locks the door behind us and starts to go to work. My phone vibrates.

Where are you? Frankie's message reads. She's been trying to reach me since our phone call. Between the speed of the vehicle and the blaring sirens, our phone call must have gotten disconnected on the way. Either that or I hung up on her in my fugue-like state.

At scene. Handling things, I send back quickly as the wall of screens flash as they all power up.

"Were just the screens off, or was it the entire system?"

"When no one's in here, we shut the screens down. The security system is always running."

"Shouldn't someone always be operating the cameras?"

"During the day, yes, but it also depends. As I said, they were shooting outside and had their own security team."

Come home, Frankie's next text pleads. I promised her before we were married I wouldn't turn into myself and shut her out. It's a hard thing to do, but right now I don't know how to handle this.

I have to go through security tapes. I need to do this; please understand. It won't be long. My thumbs swipe across my phone quickly before hitting send. A logo pops on the screen as George starts typing into a keyboard on the desk.

Okay. I'm going to take Chase to be with Mia and the kids. He needs to have family right now. He's scared. Her reply is swift, and I can tell she's unhappy with my decision but is respecting it.

Give him a hug for me. Maybe you two should stay with them for a bit. Might get crazy around town. I hope she decides to stay there for a day or two. Chase can be dropped off at school, but I'd feel better if he had a quiet place to stay.

No. He wants to sleep in our bed tonight. We'll come home. Please be safe. Her next texts flash on my watch as George types on the keyboard, pulling up the day's videos.

I'll be home late. Be safe, Meine Liebe. I sign off in my mother's native tongue. It's something I've started doing recently, giving her access to a side of myself that no one has ever had. Maybe my therapist will appreciate the steps I've taken to get healthy, or she'll laugh and ask me how that made me feel. I fucking hate psychology sometimes.

"Here we go," George interrupts as I put my phone back in its belt holster.

"When was the first shot?"

"About four hours ago. I'll start the clips about twenty minutes before-hand."

"No, start from the beginning of the day. Let's see if there's anything out of the ordinary that stands out."

"That might be a waste of time."

"It's what I can control," I say, waiting for him to set everything back to the beginning. "We can scroll through it at two-times speed. It might take a while, but we should be able to notice any glaring issues. If nothing else, the tech team will rip it apart later."

George starts the tapes, and the timecode of four a.m. pops up on the screen. The headlights of delivery trucks and some crew members walking up to the gate show on the main camera feed.

"The guard checks their pass if they're cast, crew, or authorized to be on set. For the delivery trucks, we take their license and give them a short-term pass with a number. When they leave, they turn it in, and we mark them out."

"How many of those passes are given out in one day?"

"I've had days when only two are used. During a heavy haul day, you could have up to ten. It depends on what has to be brought in, what sets need to be built, and other stuff like that."

"Pause it." George does as I ask. "Pen and paper?" He reaches under the desk to a small rolling shelving unit. After pulling out three drawers, he hands me a black pen and a small, very used steno pad. I quickly write down the time code and the plate number of the first truck. "Go ahead."

The footage continues, and we watch another truck roll in. I take down the same information as before and wait to see when they exit. About an hour later, the first truck leaves and the second one is only a few minutes after it. Two visitor passes accounted for from beginning to end.

The sun rises on the feed, and the city comes to life. The traffic outside of the lot begins to build. More cars drop people off at the location. One by one, they come to the gate, show their identification, and walk inside. Some wave to the guard, having built a friendly rapport over the shooting schedule.

A blacked-out SUV drives inside and waits at the gate. I write down the plate and timecode as a reference. After a few minutes of waiting, they proceed into the building.

"Who was that?"

"Talent. Their transportation is kept behind the fence for privacy and safety concerns."

Barricades begin to go up outside as the crew blocks off the street.

"Have you met the talent? All of them?"

"Of course. I'm the head of security. Everyone from extras to stunt doubles to the main headliners get the pleasure of getting their passes from me." George smiles sadly.

"You must have some great stories."

"My kids love them. Always asking for more than I have really, but it's fine. Never had an issue on the job beyond some eager fans. Today shook us all."

"But you should know the inner workings of everything around here."

"I know more than the average person, but even I don't have control over the schedule or who goes where. I manage my team and passes. Beyond that, it's the production company in association with the studio."

A crowd forms along the metal barricades as the crew meanders out to set things up.

"Anyone make the people disperse?"

"Sometimes, but as I said, it's out of my hands once they go off the lot."

I scan the other monitors and see an array of activity everywhere. People inside are ants running in a nest, carrying food, material for set construction, and new equipment to the other set. If it were any other situation, I'd smile at the insanity of it all. People continue to enter and exit the front gate, but no cars. The side lot has a few of the blacked-out SUVs we saw earlier in the video. Blocked off from the public, I assume that's the dedicated lot for talent and higher-up producers on the project.

A camera with a better angle of the street shows a small contingent of plainclothes individuals walking along the lines, talking to the crowd. A few minutes later, Hadley walks out with a few guards and Will behind her. She makes her way to the public and mingles with them.

"Play it real time."

George hits a few buttons, and the video returns to its original speed. Hadley walks along the metal barricades, signing autographs and taking selfies with fans. She reaches toward the back, grabs items, signs them, and hands them back. Parents in the front even lift their children to hug Disney's new darling. One by one, she ensures everyone standing outside gets an autograph if they want one. The crowd, for their part, are well-mannered and calm. There's minimal shoving in the back until Hadley reaches through; then it stops. None of the individuals show any indication of the violent act yet to come. It's all orderly.

Will stands by her side, assisting when needed or asked. He reaches over and helps a little girl in costume over the barricade. I watch as Hadley kneels and takes a few moments with her. The child's father frantically takes photos of the two of them. Hadley pulls her into a hug as the young girl appears to cry. The two spend a few more seconds together before she moves on down the line. Watching her with the people outside makes my heart swell. Hadley was bred for this line of work.

Slowly, she finishes with the crowds and waves to them all as a crew member leads them to her mark. My stomach roils as the time clicks away in the top right corner, each second bringing us closer to the shooting. The director walks up to her, and I assume they talk about the setup itself. Hadley walks through her action sequence and bounces around on her starting point. Will hugs her, then points over to the side before he walks out of the shot.

The security camera follows the scene as it unfolds. Hadley runs up the street, fights off someone, and then runs out of frame. I watch as they do it two more times while I assume they're rolling. The third take starts normally. Hadley moves forward but is thrown backward by an unseen force. In an instant, the crowd is fleeing in all directions, the entire crew rushing inside to perceived safety. Near the barricade, children are covered by their parent's bodies as others pull out their cell phones to document it. Through it all, Hadley lies on the concrete—alone.

Will scans the crowd, gun raised, trying to pinpoint where the shot came from. He turns, sees Hadley on the ground, and holsters his weapon immediately. He rushes to her side, pulling off his jacket and rolling it up into a ball before pressing it to her wound. Security personnel run outside and disperse the crowd as much as possible as they assess what's going on. Will yells to the closest one. The guard immediately pulls out his phone and, I assume, calls 911. Will continues to keep his focus on Hadley, probably to keep her awake and alert.

Several police cruisers pull into the frame, and officers jump out quickly. The first on scene rushes over to Will. The others immediately start getting a handle on the crowd, pushing them further away. The blacked-out SUVs pull out of the lot and away from the crime. The camera facing the other side of the building shows those inside fleeing out the front doors. Slowly, the street is locked down as an ambulance pulls up.

Two paramedics rush out of the vehicle and over to Hadley. Will never wavers, keeping pressure on his jacket to stem the bleeding. I watch as the two men work feverishly around my partner. An IV is in, and Hadley's vitals are recorded in what feels like record time. Carefully, they get Hadley on a backboard and strap her in before transferring her to a gurney. In about five minutes, they've got Hadley and Will and are rushing away to the hospital.

The crowd edges closer to the crime scene after the ambulance departs. Several officers try to keep the crowd back, but some climb up fire escapes to get a better vantage point. Time seems to slow as we watch the officers look around and cordon off the entire area. The process of clearing the location is arduous but necessary. After fifteen or so minutes, the mobile command unit pulls in. Zeile must have pulled some strings to get it on-site so quickly.

Another ten minutes pass as more uniformed and plainclothes officers scour the scene. I watch them work but also scan the crowd of people in the vicinity. Some of their faces are new, but no one seems out of the ordinary. The force of the bullet would lead me to believe it was a high-powered rifle, but handheld pistols can have the same effect. You can hide anything in your jacket, then fire and disappear into the chaos.

News vans show up, their satellites telescoping high into the air. Officers are holding the line as they try to get a better look at the bloodstain. Reporters stand in front of bright lights, giving an update or some hypothesis on what happened. With each passing minute, the crowd increases in size. Some people come with balloons and attach them to the studio fence. Others hold their cell phones out, but the majority hold candles in the dimming light.

Nothing seemed out of the ordinary on the first watch. The one thing I know for sure: it was only one shot that took Hadley down.

"Can you rewind to the moment before the shooting?"

George rewinds and hits play. I scan the crowd shown on the fence camera closely. The scene unfolds as before. "Again," I say. George rewinds the feed, and I choose the next spot in, focusing solely on that section. Nothing.

"Again." George continues to do as I ask, and I focus on one small section at a time, hoping to see something change or pop out at me.

"Again." I focus on the end of the line, north of where Hadley was shot. Considering what the captain told me before, I could have started here, but I needed to be thorough. It's then I see a flash of something abnormal.

"Again, but slow it down."

Frame by frame, the scene unfolds in front of me. It's then I see the unmistakable movement: a flash and something white with specks of blue before Hadley hits the ground.

"What the fuck is that?" The words exit my mouth before I can contain them. George rewinds and looks at the screen with me. He pauses it once the white and blue are noticeable.

"I have no idea, but whatever it is shows up before Ms. Moreno is shot."

I write down the timecode and a note to myself about the section. A knock on the door pulls George away from the screen, and I force myself to ignore the woman outside the door in a power suit. It's probably the warrant requesting all this footage be sent to the precinct. My eyes remain focused on the image. Whatever it is, I've never seen it before. With all those people around, no one saw anything or reacted to a gun until it was fired. I have a feeling this is important to the case, but I don't know why, and that scares the shit out of me.

Reaching for my cell phone, I snap a quick image of the screen. The distortion of the LCD screen to camera twists the colors a bit, but the unmistakable outline of a gun is still there. Sydney and the team will continue to look at the footage in a way my naked eyes can't. In the meantime, this picture is all I have to go on.

***

The house is dark and quiet when I get home. Dishes are cleaned and drying in the tray next to the sink. I walk up the stairs and see that Chase's backpack hangs over the end post of the railing, the zipper closed, homework done and checked by my wife.

Frankie and Chase rest snuggled together in the master bedroom. His hair is in desperate need of a cut, and his right arm holds onto Frankie's. Her hair is laid out like an angel's breath swept it across her pillow. In this moment, my room holds the most precious and beautiful parts of my life. Part of me wonders if another child is in our future. With so much love to give, maybe that's something I'm ready to consider. Well, that and a larger bed so the kids won't kick us so hard.

Knowing that sleep will not be coming soon, I head back to the kitchen to look over the current files. I grab a beer from the fridge and sit and stare at my cell phone. Flipping open my tablet case, I quickly begin a search for weapons with varying color schemes or available paint modifications in the search parameters. The main responses refer to skins or paint themes for video game weaponry. Nothing of relevance, but interesting to note nonetheless. If the individual had a real weapon and painted it, maybe the theme they used for the paint job could lead us back to their video game character or some digital connection.

My God. I sound like Logan. He would be so much faster at this though. He'd know how someone managed to pick up his pizza. He'd already have an image of the person who came to his door. Logan would have used all the power the internet had to offer to give us a lead. Instead, I am holding, waiting, and praying. Sydney is tech-savvy and probably even better than the current second-in-command, but she's not Logan. No one is.

My instincts tell me there was only one shot fired based on video evidence. I can't be one hundred percent certain without the sound, but the reaction of Hadley's body gives me all I need for now. I search for colorful, single-fire weapons, and the list is confusing.

Toy guns from Mattel and Fisher-Price. Orange tips that still looking like real weapons that can be converted to fully functional with a few tweaks. Schematics on how to convert regular pipes into a blow dart-type gun. Blood bullets, ice bullets, all kinds of modifications to the ammunition to make it more deadly or less traceable. All the sites house disclaimers stating a lack of evidence to prove their theories or that the information provided is for education only. They never advise using the blueprints or trying this at home. It's the bullshit cop-out of the century when handing people information on how to kill. We would still prosecute the person for screaming fire in a crowded room, even if he made a disclaimer that it "may or may not be an actual fire." Like I said: a bullshit cop-out.

One search result causes my eyes to stop their quick scan. *Liberator Pistol, download, print, shoot,* the headline read along with an image of a blue, toy-looking gun. Opening the link, the CNN article discusses the current state of affairs within our administration and the fight over background checks. Scanning further, it shows the same bright blue pistol and the caption *No one can trace it. No background checks. No way to stop production.*

3D printing of guns is a very gray area in this country. There's no way to stop them since they seem to pass through metal detectors. They can be made at home or in the office if you have time and privacy. Depending on the blueprints, which are now freely available online, you can have several pistols ready to go. You only get one shot, but so much damage can be done with one bullet. Then you walk away, blending in with the crowd as you dismantle the weapon and throw it away.

It's perfect. It's easy, and it is very difficult for the police to detect. Looking back at the image with the white and blue colors, I conclude the weapon was printed in plastic. I don't know whether to be thankful it only had one shot or to be concerned about the possibility of more attacks. Either way, this person has the means to kill everyone—one bullet at a time.

Chapter Eight

I leave a note for Frankie in the morning, explaining I slept on the couch because Chase was too stubborn to move his feet from my side of the bed. She'll hopefully laugh at that thought and tell me all about it later. Maybe they slept late this morning and had a fun breakfast. I needed to come in early and keep the information flowing through my veins.

On the right side of the large whiteboard—my mind-mapping tool from my probationary officer days—I've taped a printed copy of the security footage image, with the words "3D printed gun" with a section about the Liberator pistol underneath it. I'm not sure it is that specific gun, but it is a good reference point for this case. I stand and tap a dry erase marker against the board to the beat of an eighties song and think.

Pages of suspects litter my desk. The prospects range from a high school student to an old white man who has a history of prostitution arrests. They could be fans, sickos, or something more sinister. Then there's the dark forum Thomas brought up. He said the names on the list were a part of it, but to what extent and if they procured anything is up to Sydney to figure out.

"Detective?" A woman's voice from behind causes me to spin, drop the marker, and almost lose my balance.

"Yes?"

"I'm Morgan Lancaster. I'll be handling prosecuting all the cases that come out of this office." She extends her hand, which I immediately shake.

"I don't know if that's a promotion or demotion."

"I don't just handle this office. It's part of the job and the new title."

"Not a new paycheck though, right?" The words mesh with laughter as I sit on the edge of my desk. "Sorry, that's rude of me. It just seems like when you work for a nonprofit or the government, you're given fancy titles without the financial support to go with it."

She leans against Karina's desk as she talks. Her gray power suit clings to her in all the right places and shows off her well-toned physique. The way she carries herself borders on intimidating. Her dark eyes feel as if they see through you directly to your soul. Her bright red nail polish contrasts with her black skin.

"Not rude at all, detective." She smiles while looking at the ceiling. "I can promise you some of us do what we love for justice over paychecks. It's still nice to get a bump every now and again, though, isn't it?"

"Very much so. Do you prefer Ms. or is there a different . . ."

"Morgan is fine. Would you mind if I call you Jasmine? I prefer being on a first-name basis. It makes things feel less formal and more approachable. Unless you have a preferred nickname?"

"That's fine."

"Good, now onto business. Have you gotten any closer to the assailant behind these two attacks? Before you try to dissuade me, I know a single perpetrator when we have one. I also know your colleague is looking over the security footage as we speak. If there were two individuals, we would have some indication by now."

"Okay," I answer, letting my brain process everything. "Currently, we're not much further along than we were yesterday. Not for lack of trying," I reply, not sure if Morgan has clearance to hear my hunches or Google search results.

"You think the weapon was digitally printed," she says, looking over my notes on the whiteboard. "That's both unique and frightening."

"And it's currently a theory with no factual basis at this time, Morgan." Karina's firm voice is heard from the doorway, and she enters the fray.

"Karina, I was checking in to see what I could assist with. Nothing more." The smooth tone in Morgan's voice is in stark disparity to her sly smirk.

"I appreciate that, but we've got it handled. If any member of my team has a lead to share, I'll call you personally."

Morgan grabs her purse and opens the door leading to the stairs. "You've had things handled before, Karina. Just don't be blinded by what's right in front of you this time, okay, dear?" She swings the door to the emergency stairs open wide before walking through, her heels clickity clicking on the metal floor as her afro bounces with each step before it closes shut behind her.

"You don't share any information with her until it's been cleared by me or the captain, understand?" Karina's angry tone rips into me.

"Okay, first, I didn't share anything. She came in here of her own accord and read my notes. I can't stop how I work through a case because someone wants to scan my notes. Secondly, she happens to be a member of our legal team. That indicates she's on our side. If I need to bounce something off her in regard to the legal aspects of the case, I will," I answer quickly. "Finally, what the hell has crawled up your ass lately? I'm trying to be patient, but it's reaching an all-time high and pissing me off."

"Contact Morgan directly and I'll send your ass back to the Bronx for overnight shifts. She's not one of us, and it would behoove you to remember that." She slams her fist against her desk to end the conversation. Ignoring her outburst, I look back over the board, and my hand shakes holding the marker. Therapy is going to be fun later.

"What was she talking about?" Karina switches topics, trying to bring it back to something more professional. "The printed gun. Where did you get that connection from?"

"I noticed something odd watching the footage from the scene. George, the security guard, went frame by frame, and the shot came from the north side of the barricades. Now, we assumed this based on how Hadley fell, but no one saw a weapon. So far, we have no witnesses coming forward with any useful information. Watching the frames, I noticed this shape that was blue and white. Now, I know it sounds out of left field, but if it were plastic, no one would be the wiser. There'd be a noise, recoil, and maybe a spark; information is spotty online about that. The point is, it acts like a weapon, but it's easier to hide, harder to detect, and much simpler to dispose of."

"That theory assumes someone could afford all the equipment necessary to build it."

"Or have access to it. Local colleges carry these types of printers for scientific purposes. I doubt they have logs for used cartridges considering how many mistakes can be made at any given time."

"Leaving an even thinner trail to follow."

"Precisely. So, maybe we need to look into these individuals and see who does what."

"I think we should speak to everyone regardless," Karina says. "Maybe having the FBI knock on their door will give them pause from attacking someone on social media again."

"Or they'll rage against the swamp, feed into conspiracy theories and ignorance."

"The law is against us, Steele. Right now, all we have is stalking at best and nuisance at worst."

"Attempted murder."

"While I agree that these two attacks are most likely connected, we have to think about proving it beyond a reasonable doubt. What's the connection? What evidence do we have that it's the same individual? If you have it, we can easily arrest them, process paperwork, and be home in time for a nice glass of wine. Not to mention 3D-printed guns are notoriously inaccurate at hitting their targets. We're pushing the boulder uphill here, Jasmine. Let's focus on what we do have: grainy images of a man in a trucker hat with what may or may not be the weapon in question."

"Karina, at least . . ." My cell phone vibrates on the table, stopping our conversation dead. My heart races as I look at my watch, praying it isn't Will with bad news. Thankfully, it's Dr. Brown. demanding my presence immediately. "It's Lil. I have to go see what forensics came up with. We might not have a lot, Karina, but this is how it goes. We either fight as a team or maybe this position isn't right for you."

I expect a harsh reply, but instead, I see a broken woman leaning over her desk. For the first time since she reemerged in my life, I notice her wedding ring is missing. The only time she ever took it off was to go undercover, and even then, it was attached to something in her undergarments. She always felt connected to reality, to her family, when the thin gold band was there.

"I'll keep you posted on the doc's info. Maybe you should check in with Sydney. She's been working on that forum angle."

She doesn't respond verbally, just waving her hand in acceptance. I make a mental note to talk to her when this is all over. If we're going to be working together long term, we need to clear the air of whatever grievances she might have. The Garrison case was huge for her as well. Maybe things got out of hand or her bosses weren't thrilled with how we solved it. Maybe her job became too much and her marriage suffered. No matter what the reason, if she stays, she's part of our work family, and that means we have to support her. Maybe the rumors about her husband were true. If he's the Seattle Slayer, her entire world would be turned on its head.

***

It always feels like I'm walking through a trendy area of Manhattan when I navigate the forensic teams' hallways. Dr. Brown, fashionable as ever, stares into a microscope in one of the side labs, hair pulled back in a tight bun, glasses perched at the edge of her nose as she frantically writes information down. As I knock on the glass, she turns to me and presses a small button under the desk, which opens the door.

"New locks?"

"I like my privacy, Steele. You know this."

"Smaller lab than before."

"Well, this new department requires a ton of reevaluating paper and previous results. That means downsizing and more delegating for me."

"Sorry, I know you'd rather be in the thick of things."

"Don't be. I get to be more attentive to detail and choose the cases I need to be focused on. They also allowed me to hire two new staff members, so no harm, no foul." She spins around and walks back to the center table, which holds a monitor on a posable arm and a keyboard. I assume the computer is in the cabinet locked away from casual usage.

"You demanded my presence up here?"

"I requested firmly, Steele. I'm nothing if not polite." She taps on the keyboard in front of her, and when finished, she turns the monitor around for me to view. "I did want you to see this before I put out the formal report to the captain and Agent Marlow."

"What am I looking at?"

"There was a ton of evidence in Logan's apartment ranging from simple dust to sheets that should have been cleaned. Don't get me started on the age of the mattress or pillows. Dust mites and dead skin galore."

"Lil, please get to the point."

"Everything was as expected. Pizza appeared as one would expect initially. When I did further testing on the sauce and cheese, I found large amounts of krill oil."

"Okay, so the kid likes shrimp on his pie even though it is beyond disgusting and rivals pineapple as the worst topping."

"Not precisely shrimp. Krill oil is found in various over-the-counter tablets like fish oils or glucosamine and chondroitin for joints. The FDA doesn't regulate them, so some companies add a higher percentage of krill per gel capsule. There was enough of it mixed into the pizza to cause a massive allergic reaction."

"This is where you tell me Logan is allergic to shellfish."

"According to his medical records, deathly. He can't have it touch his skin without breaking out in a massive rash that could cover his body in seconds."

"Wouldn't he be able to taste the difference?"

"Normally, I would say yes, but he finished the majority of the pie. I have to assume he either didn't taste it, was so hungry he didn't care about the off-putting taste, or . . ."

"He was also actively playing video games with friends," I say. "I doubt he'd want to get up to use the bathroom, let alone stop eating. There are only so many breaks during campaign missions. His attention was acutely focused elsewhere."

"Could have been biological as well; when we're in stressful situations, or perceived ones, our chemical composition changes. Logan might have experienced an altered gustation."

"Are you sure about this?"

"One hundred percent. After the tests, I wanted to wait for the toxicology report to confirm it before reporting to the higher-ups. I also asked for a histamine level exam. Both confirm my findings. The only way to be surer is if I had his stomach contents to prove he ate the food."

"Evidence on his hands, mouth, and throat all corroborate your findings?"

"Yes. Do you doubt me?"

"No, doc, but this means someone had access to Logan's files."

"Maybe not." Lillian flips the monitor around quickly before typing again. After a few seconds of waiting, she turns the screen back. There is an extreme close-up of a black medical bracelet. It reads: *Allergy Penicillin & Shellfish*. Clear as day. "Hadley bought it for him after their first date. She had lobster, and his hand broke out into hives from holding hers later that evening. He needed to go to the hospital. His file said he was given Pepcid, steroids, and a Benadryl drip. Anyone with a computer could find these images and magnify it to a readable level."

"I never noticed him wearing it."

"I noticed it when we all went out for our monthly dinner. Hadley was adamant he put it on."

"Why didn't I notice that?"

"Jasmine, you've been busy with everything going on at work and home. It's natural to miss things like this."

"No, it's not." The harsh words flow out of my mouth before I can stop them. "Send the report to Marlow and Zeile. I'm going to check in with Syd, see if she found anything else. Did you tell the hospital?"

"Yes, they now know the exact allergen, but they treated it like any other severe allergic reaction."

"Give me the truth, Lil. How bad is it?"

"His brain was without oxygen for a short time. It might be nothing, could be worse. The bigger concern is the swelling on his brain. The histamine levels are slowly coming down, but not fast enough for any doctor's liking. As I said, this could all be moot when he wakes up."

"But?"

"His brain could say that little drought was enough to shut everything down. It could just stop functioning altogether."

"Over a shellfish allergy?"

"His throat swelled shut while his tongue swelled outward. It wasn't just an allergy. There's a reason he has EpiPens in his emergency kit."

"Then why didn't he use them?"

"They found Benadryl next to him. I assume he thought that would stop the reaction before it became critical. EpiPens are a last resort. You have to go to the hospital once you use them. Maybe he was leery of them? I don't know, Jasmine. I just know why he's in the hospital and the ramifications of that event. I focus on the science, not speculation. That's your department." The words come out of her mouth like a wave smashing into your back on the beach. "I'm sorry. I shouldn't have said that. I'm just concerned."

"No worries. We're all a bit on edge right now," I say, trying to quell the tension in the room. "Thanks for the updates. Keep me posted on the evidence from the scene this morning."

My feet take me to the other end of the room before I hear Lillian walking behind me. "Lil?"

"I just . . . Make sure they don't tell her. She'll blame herself."

"I know, but she has to survive first." The somberness of my mood seeps into my words as I leave the floor and head to the garage. I have an appointment with my therapist again today. Twice a week I have to see her, but Frankie gave me three sessions this week. She even put two of them back to back. Maybe she knew I would avoid the first one and fight it all. Normally I'd skip it, but today I need the solace.

***

Staring out into the oasis of trees intermingling with cement and grass, my mind wishes for the clarity of childhood, running through crowds, my mother yelling behind me, no care in the world. The perceived feeling of invincibility and immortality was such a novel concept back then. But time moves on, and we grow up. Sipping the hot peppermint tea Dr. Preston made for me has helped calm my nerves somewhat. I've never been one for therapy in any capacity—ironic considering my masters in the field.

"How's your tea?" She cuts into my inner monologue and pulls me back to reality. I'm thankful she's waited for some time before breaking me from my thoughts. The calm here has helped me focus somewhat.

"Nice, thank you."

"You left before our session ended last time. I honestly didn't expect you to return for today's meeting."

"It's quiet here, and I need that to think."

"It's also a place to work things through. I'm sure your stress level has increased recently."

"You've been paying attention to the news."

"It's hard not to, but we don't have to discuss anything or everything. It's really up to you."

"I don't want to hear the usual psychologist crap. I don't want you to utter the words "how does that make you feel." Agreed? We're having conversations, like old college friends. That's the only way this is going to work."

"As you wish." She sips her coffee before leaning back in her chair. "How are you holding up, given the circumstances?"

"How's this whole situation make me feel, you mean?" I let out a sarcastic laugh that fills the room. "I told you not to ask that."

"I didn't. You interpreted it as such. As your college buddy, I want to know how you are currently doing."

"I'm fighting a losing battle." I continue to stare into the park, avoiding eye contact. "It's the main issue with stalking. We can't do anything or search anywhere. There's no evidence other than this online shit we found, and what use is that? People can hide behind fake names and say they didn't mean it. I can't prove intent, so it's all just useless. Everything is tied up *and* fucked up until something major happens. By then . . ."

I take another sip, trying to control my heart racing in my chest. "We could have prevented Logan from being poisoned and Hadley from being shot. None of this was necessary if she had come forward sooner."

"What could be done if she had?"

"I don't know. Maybe I'd have gotten her more security, found all those little shits online and had lawyers send letters or something. Hell, maybe Had would be taking it upon herself to talk to the politicians and get the laws changed. There might have been options we didn't have before it all went to hell."

"Did she have protection?"

"Yeah, the studio hired security during filming due to some secrecy around the production. There was security on set, and she had my partner by her side once we knew what was going on. He was there when she was shot. Probably saved her life."

"Then it sounds like you did everything possible within the constraints of the law and your position," she says, sipping her coffee.

Letting the words sink in, I stay quiet as my body drops into the chair opposite the doc. "There's always more that can be done. You have to know where to look. The team's been scouring every possible angle, but it's as if there's nothing there. We're all grasping at straws."

"Well, forgive me, dear college friend, but how does that make you feel?"

"Seriously?" I sip more of my tea before thinking of a proper answer. "I hate that fucking question. It's like you expect this profound response, but all I can say truthfully is I don't fucking know. It's not about me or my inability to break through the red tape of bullshit this time. It's about my friends lying in hospital beds and useless me hoping they live."

"Your inability to break through the red tape? I don't quite understand that."

"I promised Frankie that I wouldn't be running halfcocked anymore. I'd do things by the book regardless of my instincts or gut feelings. I have a family of my choosing, and I have to be around for them. So, no more "throwing myself into the void" to solve a case."

"And this was a common behavior before?"

"People who think they have nothing to live for don't quite understand the value of life until they face death. Even then, they fight against their insecurities until they are hurt with the loss of someone who made the world brighter." I whisper this, more to myself, but the doc must have heard.

"That's beautiful. Who said it?"

"My oma." I say the German word before translating. "Grandmother."

"She sounds like a smart woman."

"She was. That, and so much more."

"Want to tell me about her?"

My cell phone vibrates, and I pull it out to stare at the screen. With an apologetic expression to the doc, I answer Frankie. "Baby, I'm in my session."

"I know, but this was important. You need to get to the hospital now."

"Is it Hadley?"

"It's Logan." Her voice lowers. "Jasmine, full sirens."

She disconnects the call, and fear settles in my stomach. I don't say anything to Jenette as I grab my things and fumble to get out of the door. I can hear her behind me, asking questions, but if I open my mouth, bile will come rushing out. I need to get to my wife. I need to get to my family.

Chapter Nine

Hospitals: the place people go to get healthy or die. There's no real middle ground. You either walk out on your own, or you go to the morgue, hospice, or worse yet—rehab. I remember my grandfather hopped back and forth from the rehab facility to the hospital like a ping-pong ball. He couldn't move, someone stole his dentures, and the entire medical facility passed the buck. He could check out and get new ones, but that would absolve them of responsibility. I think that's why he signed a DNR. To him, death was a better option over negligence, greed, and indifferent care. To this day, my heart screams that the hospital killed his will to live and therefore murdered him. We should have sued everyone involved, but my oma wanted to put the past behind her. I added the hospital to my toe tag list. Dead is the only way I'm going in that door.

Rushing through the front corridor, my body feels like it's moving in slow motion as my mind plays the worst scenarios over and over. The first security guard demands to see my badge and calls up to verify my credentials. The crowd moves around me to the second guard, who stares at the identification cards and moves on. This is taking too long.

My badge hits my palm, and I'm running to catch an elevator before it closes. The tenth floor is usually a flurry of activity but seems slower as my feet hit the linoleum tiles in a full sprint out of the elevator and down the hall to the area housing my friends. My legs awkwardly stop, my knees screaming at the motion as several uniformed officers come into view, hats on, thumbs hooked into their belts as their backs press into the wall. Not one of them raises their head as I walk by.

"Jasmine." Frankie stands in front of me, her face unreadable and cut off. Her arms are wrapped protectively around her midsection as if holding herself together.

"Frankie, what's going on."

She says nothing as she reaches for my hand. Our fingers mesh together as seamlessly as they always have before she pulls me down the corridor to the last room on the right. Captain Zeile stands facing the window, his hands stuffed in his pants pockets. Two doctors argue in muffled tones on the other side of the room. Logan lies in the bed, still and unmoving. His skin is ashen. His body is thinner than it was just a few days ago. The silence is what catches my attention immediately.

"Why are the machines off?" My voice echoes loudly, and I hear it rebound down the hallway. Frankie closes the door, stopping the commotion inside from reaching the officers.

"They're not totally off, honey, just the sound. I promise," Frankie says, rubbing her free hand up and down my arm.

"Why turn the sound off? I'm not a doctor, but I know the sound is always on in this shithole. Fuck, everyone complains that they can't heal because of the incessant beeping or overhead announcements!"

"Detective, your associates brought you here because of your connection to Ms. Moreno."

"What he's trying to say is that Hadley has you listed as her medical proxy."

"She what? I mean, when? Why would she?"

"I don't know, and right now we can't ask her, but Logan has no family we can contact, and you were given legal rights by Hadley."

"They want you to make decisions for Logan's care," Zeile says from the window, his calm demeanor causing my hair to stand up on end.

"Is that even legal?" I ask.

"Hadley is listed as Mr. Pevy's medical proxy. We hoped since you were hers, there might have been a conversation about . . ."

"About what? How the hell to handle a one-in-a-million scenario where both of them are out? Seriously?"

"Jasmine, you were close to Logan."

"Will was closer," I counter.

"Maybe, but you are the one who can make the decision. I don't think he can."

"He's a former Marine; they eat difficult decisions for lunch."

"Steele, we don't have time. It was my call, and I made it," Zeile answers firmly.

I look at Logan in the bed again, then at Frankie and back to the doctors. I feel Frankie's fingers lace with mine for moral support.

"What's going on?" I ask the two doctors, my hand squeezing Frankie's for strength.

"Mr. Pevy has been progressing positively until this morning. He had several small seizures in a row, and his brain activity has decreased significantly. We need to consider the possibility—"

"That you will continue doing anything and everything that medical science can provide to save him, yes. You're abso-fucking-lutely right. Until his body gives out, you keep working. Until the power on the respirator is blown up by some act of God, you keep him alive."

"Jasmine, we need to consider his quality of life," Frankie says.

"I am. Until he gives me a sign that he is ready to go, we fight. He's had a few seizures. So what. That could be caused by anything. So, let them continue giving him fluids, antibiotics, or what have you. Run some tests, see if there's pressure or something. Figure out the cause and then handle it. I'm letting them do what they get paid to do."

"Okay," Frankie says. She kisses our joined hands.

"You heard her. Run whatever tests you need." Zeile turns around, his face dark with exhaustion. "I'll make sure they do everything, Steele. You might want to check in next door."

Frankie leads me across the hall and into a room with all the electronic noises of a typical hospital room. The beeping brings calm to my jagged nerves. Will notices us in the doorway and is holding me in his arms before I can protest.

"Thank you," he whispers in my ear, and I know instantly he heard the commotion next door.

"You'd do the same."

"I don't know if I could. If I had these kinds of supplies in the desert . . ." He pulls back from the embrace and looks me dead in the eye. "I would have kept every one of my brothers alive."

I feel the sincerity of his words as I look over his shoulder to Hadley's prone form. She appears to be dreaming as her eyes bounce around. In some way that comforts me; if they're moving, it means she has brain activity. She looks so small and weak in the larger bed. Nothing like the Hadley I know.

"How is she?"

"Lost a lot of blood, but there was no shortage of donors. Surgery went well. The bullet was removed with her appendix. She'll have a wicked scar, but she's lucky. The rest is up to her."

"Can I have a moment?"

Frankie and Will leave me alone with Hadley. Her paler-than-normal skin shocks me a bit. It's almost too much to process: the wires connecting her to the machines and intravenous fluids, the breathing tube forcing her chest to rise and fall systematically. Her hand, warm enough to be alive but colder than her normal temperature, falls into mine.

I press her knuckles to my forehead as I sit in the chair by the bed. In my head, I try and tell myself this is her stunt double. It all makes sense. The facts all line up properly. She is almost an identical twin and could fool any fan. The old camera feeds were grainy and not as clear as a newer one would be. The captain prevented me from seeing her or working on her case. It all fits the bigger puzzle. Hadley is fine, and her double is here in this bed. I just have to play along.

The guilt boils over as a few tears escape my eyes. Both of them are someone's daughter, friend, partner, or sister. Neither one deserves to be in this bed, yet I wish—no *beg*—for it to be someone other than my Hadley.

It's an odd thing, wishing another would take her place. I'm not thinking about the human element of this type of grief. There was a time recently Hadley wanted to take my place. She was still struggling then, felt I had more to live for. I had a family, a career, and a future. She's selfless, and the rest of us are selfish.

In this age of access, people don't understand boundaries. They push and complain when someone doesn't reply to an email, post, or text. It's as if the world revolves around only one person and their demands. It used to be that only killers, rapists, and corrupt government officials were so public about it. The more advanced we get, the more backward we trend.

I have no doubt the public's obsession with fame and notoriety led to Hadley lying in this bed. News media will say the law is slow to catch up, but the law is created by old men living off the public trough. Their ideals are out of touch with humanity and civility, yet they remain. Until that changes, my friend will continue to be stalked like the ice cream man in summer.

"I'm so sorry, Had." The words fall from my mouth before the silent shaking sobs wrench through my body. My tangential are thoughts lost to the fear as I feel Frankie wrap her arms around me. Her perfume fills my senses as my shoulder dampens with her tears. It's the most emotion she's seen from me in years.

"I've got you." Her whispers hit my ears, and my free hand pulls her in tighter.

***

Pulling up to St. Luke's Roosevelt Hospital, I throw my police placard on the dash as Karina knocks on the passenger side glass.

"How'd you get here?"

"Subway. Not everyone wants to drive in this shit," she replies, pointing to the cars backed up on Tenth Avenue.

"Thought the feds gave you one."

"Case-by-case basis." She grabs the handle and holds it open for me to walk into the lobby. "Zeile called. You good?"

"Still above ground," I answer flatly. Karina seems to accept this as she continues her way through the lobby. Reaching the front desk, a woman shoves a clipboard forward with a pen hanging from a red ribbon.

"Ma'am, I'm looking—"

"Sign in and we'll call you up," she says, her accent thick and difficult to understand as she refuses to look up from the papers in front of her.

"I'm not injured. We're here to see—"

"Sign in and you can see the staff on hand."

My badge slams against the counter, forcing the nurse to turn her attention to us. "Is that supposed to mean something? Sign in," she replies before tossing my badge back at me. Karina holds her FBI identification out, and the woman scans it. "You have a bigger badge. Congrats. Sign in."

"We're investigating a case and need to speak to Liz Gentri. She's a nurse here," Karina says.

"Sign in and I'll let her know you're here." She scans the ID again. "Agent Marlow."

I would love to sign the German word for asshole on the sheet, but I put both our names instead. *Jasmine, you must always carry yourself at the highest standard, it's who we Steele women are.* My mother's voice rattles around the synaptic responses in my brain.

The receptionist grabs the phone and waves us to the waiting area of the emergency room, and the hard plastic chairs that hurt more than they help. The kids are wiping noses on their parents' shirts or hands before touching everything in sight. The two of us, having raised kids ourselves, stand off to the side. It's second nature to avoid little petri dishes of disease.

"Agent Marlow?" A woman with a tight bun and pink scrubs stands by the main doors.

"Liz Gentri?" Karina asks.

"Yes, I was told you were looking for me."

"Is there somewhere we can talk?"

"Can you tell me what this is about?"

"It's an ongoing investigation, so we would prefer to speak somewhere with fewer ears," I add, looking around at the full waiting room.

"Of course."

The nurse leads us through the maze of beds and people to a small office. She leans against a desk and squeezes the edges.

"Now, can you please tell me what's this about?"

"We're investigating the attack on Hadley Moreno," I say.

"I was headed to my shift when it happened," she answers quickly. I would do the same thing. It's a defense mechanism when the person thinks they're being accused of a crime. If there was a manual for police investigations, the number one thing people do first is to divert attention or provide an "it wasn't me" statement. In my experience, they do it before they even know what you're asking—a pure, primal instinct to protect themselves.

"You said some rather crude things online to Ms. Moreno for over two years. Is there a reason for this animosity?"

"Are you kidding me?" the nurse starts, forcing air out of her lungs in a huff as she shakes her head. "She's a freaking whore. I used to act in some bit parts with her, but she gets the bigger roles. She's not that talented either. The only way she was getting jobs was because the director loved her tits. So yeah, I let her know it."

"So, you threatened her online because you failed as an actor instead of being happy that she succeeded?" I say. "That sounds like a motive to me. What do you think, Agent Marlow?"

"I know you. You're that cop who loves her. She fucking you too?" Gentri says, moving into my personal space.

In that split second, I could see myself closing the gap even more and screaming at her. I want to smack the smirk off her face as I break her teeth. My emotions are high, and I shove my hands in my pockets to prevent myself from going out of line.

"Ms. Gentri, if you want to make accusations on the record, we'd be happy to listen," Karina says. "Until then, have your superiors send us your timesheets for the entire month."

"Why the whole month?"

"Because this is an ongoing investigation, and we will need all pertinent information."

"I'll call a lawyer."

"You are legally allowed to do so. I can call your employer if you prefer. They should have no issue with our request." Karina hands the stunned nurse her card and walks out of the office.

Hot on her heels, I am taken aback by Karina's behavior. She interjected herself into the argument, defended me, and insisted on more information than we need to be a pain. Considering the past few days, I feel like I am walking on eggshells with her.

The traffic hasn't let up, but the weather has changed. Darker clouds have rolled in, and the breeze pushing through the canyons has a bite as rain begins to fall. Finding the comfort of my car, Karina jumps in the passenger side.

"That was a shit interrogation," I say.

"She said she has an alibi. We'll have Sydney check it out and go from there. Until then, we keep talking to people." She pulls out a small notepad and crosses out another name on her list. "The six people that I showed you before your trip to Long Island? One was Randall Cunning, a lovely sixty-year-old white male who believes that women of all ages will still service him. He has a lovely collection of porn out for the viewing public. That includes some screen captures of a specific actress in a horror film. He does send her messages on Facebook, as that's where he and his sex buddies get to virtually 'hang out.'"

I start laughing before I can stop myself. "Okay, he did not say that."

"Oh yes, he explained that his walker helps with stability. He can't drive or walk, so I quickly left to shower with Brillo before I went to see Ivan Topiz. That kid is something else. He's a thirteen-year-old math and science genius. Family is normal, all overachieving individuals. I assure you he will not have any internet access for anything other than school for a long time. His parents were none too thrilled with their kid's involvement."

"Sounds like you've had a very interesting two days."

"Yes, well Sydney ruled out a few people, which made it easier. Stephanie Chalk, rude and cruel, but her cell phone pinged in Virginia, and her Instagram corroborates her location. Hank Boner—real name Mark Hucek—is very active on the website forums, but he was in Atlantic City with receipts. Which I collected, and, no, I refused to touch them. I had him put them in a bag for me. Dr. Brown is looking them over. You spoke to Thomas Catz, and we've handled Liz Gentri."

"So, you've ruled out everyone but this last guy." I lean over to look at the pad. "Gary Barrett?"

"Sydney is working with Morgan to bring down all those within the forums for distribution of child pornography, among other things. People like Hucek and Cunning will have to face her, and I don't envy them." She pulls her seatbelt and clicks it into place. "Barrett may be our guy, but even still, we have nothing to hold him on. The footage from the pizza place is grainy. Logan's building has security footage. Surprisingly, no one else ordered pizza that night and the delivery person is pretty clear. Couldn't make out a face, but height and build was documented. Could be similar to the individual we noted on the studio security cameras. We need more. Ballistics is looking at the bullet, and hopefully, that will prove or disprove your theory. Until then, we just talk to the guy."

"You got all that in two days."

"It's called work, Steele. It's what I do."

"Yeah, but when do you sleep? See your kids?"

Her shoulders straighten, and her jaw clenches. My assumptions about her marriage must not be far off.

"They're staying with my parents in Queens. Now, shall we?"

***

One-Hundredth and Amsterdam is a row of apartment buildings with an actual parking lot. I don't know what their rent is, but people must be in heaven here. Granted, it only holds about fifteen cars, the spaces are numbered, so you have to pay, and it's across the street from a precinct fire station combo . . . but it's *parking*—in the city.

"Can you stop drooling over the lot and let's go?"

Karina buzzes apartment 16F.

"Yeah," the speaker crackles.

"Mr. Barrett, my name is Agent Marlow with the FBI. I was wondering if we could speak to you for a minute."

"Why would the FBI want to speak to me? You're no better than ICE. I don't have to speak to you."

"We're just here for some information. Nothing more."

"Then ask your questions."

"Sir, this is an ongoing investigation. For obvious reasons, we can't do as you ask."

"You want to come in, get a warrant. Until then, have a wonderful day, agent."

Karina stands unfettered and walks outside and back to the car. I hit my fob's open button, and she hops inside.

"You're in charge. What do you want to do?"

"We wait. He's got to go to work sometime."

I recline the seat and get more comfortable. I shoot Frankie a text about the spontaneous stakeout and tell her to grab Chase and keep me posted on everything. I hate not being home, but this needs to be handled.

"The great Jasmine Steele I knew would never give control to someone else. She was always in the lead of her army."

"The Karina Marlow I know never attacked those who were on her side," I counter.

"Looks like you got one while I was melting mine down," she says, rubbing her left ring finger. "Morgan and I never got along, you know. Respected each other for our accomplishments, but she has a way about her that just doesn't mesh with me," Karina begins softly. I can see her struggle to find her words on a difficult subject. "She was with the FBI for some time. She made a big enough name for herself with larger cases other attorneys were afraid to touch. Her reputation eventually allowed her to pick and choose whatever case she wanted to tackle. She chose the Seattle Slayer and moved to Washington to take over my case."

"I remember the FBI touting they solved two major cases within a year. They took a rather large victory lap."

"They did, and I was shipped out here after being cleared."

"Karina, I've read recaps and heard the rumors, but I know a lot of that is misrepresenting the truth. What happened?"

She looks through the front windshield, arms around her chest for warmth and comfort. I turn the car on, flip the heat to the max temperature, and click the heated seat button. The low buzzing of the fan drowns out the cars outside.

"I'm sure those reports left out a lot of information. Most of it is classified," she says, exhaling slowly. "I missed the evidence. It was sitting right there, buried under my master bathroom vanity. My hours were so erratic that I never really had time to take care of the house, let alone my kids. Simon, he always made sure things were clean, kids fed . . . He seemed like a supporting father and husband."

I turn my attention out the front windshield as well. Having someone stare at you while you talk about the worst moments of your life doesn't have a calming effect. In my experience, it makes matters so much worse, and you skip over things you need to get off your chest.

"There was a hidden compartment underneath the cleaning chemicals and spare toilet paper. I remember Simon lined all the shelves in the kitchen and bathrooms after we renovated years ago. He told me it was to protect our investment. Now I know it was to create uniformity so that I wouldn't see the outline of his hatches." She fights to calm her breathing, and I hand her my reusable water bottle. She twists the top off and takes a sip. Her hands keep it propped against her thighs, open and accessible.

"He had a binder with these plastic sleeves for baseball cards, I think. Inside each one was a small, sealed bag with a fingernail. Nothing was written on them, but this small, one-inch, three-ring binder was full. It made me want to vomit."

The papers never mentioned the evidence or where it was hidden. Just that Simon had taken a piece of every victim and that they were still doing DNA on some of them. He was convicted in Washington of ten counts of first-degree murder, but other states were looking into him.

"They thought I protected him at first."

I turn to face her with that comment. "They had to know that wasn't true."

"They didn't, and I don't blame them. He was my cold case I couldn't catch—the one perp who was always one step ahead of my team. They felt I must have been sharing information with him. Simon was my husband after all, and my name had been all over, connected with yours. They felt I didn't want the negative press."

"That isn't you," I mutter softly.

"You don't know me very well, Jasmine. Hell, I don't know me. Maybe I did know it was him and refused to accept it. The late-night school meetings, traveling basketball team, and other excuses to go into the city. I never questioned him or his loyalty to our marriage." Her left thumb rubs her bare ring finger. "I always locked my office, but never my files or my computer. I always left the case files at headquarters—nothing classified ever came home—but my notes, my thoughts were there. He'd know when I'd get a call to go to a scene. Simon knew everything I was doing and how to counter it. He made me look like an accomplice."

"To cover his tracks," I start, and she turns to look at me, confused. "Think about it; if he makes you look like you've been covering up for his crime, he can trade you for a lesser deal. In his mind, that might have been worth it."

"Morgan would have done that." Her eyes move back to the small courtyard in front of us. "She wanted to have me arrested. She was so damn adamant that I had to have some knowledge of the crimes happening right under my nose. As if I would live . . . let my children live with a monster like that." Her voice cracks, and she takes another sip of water. "He'd go to a bar and find the person who suited his needs, man or woman. Then he'd rape and murder them and post their bodies in public places. Then he'd come home, store his souvenir, and climb into bed with me. Sometimes, he'd . . ." She stops, but I know what she means. He'd come home and be intimate with her.

"The amount of testing, polygraphs, and interrogations was humiliating. I lost all credibility with my team and my department. My friends cut me off; the school expelled my sons because of the backlash from parents. I was suspended indefinitely."

"But you still managed to help Sydney with the Keets case. How?"

"Suspended does not deny access to computer files. I just found information and told her who to call. I asked her to keep my name out of it but never told her why."

"How'd you end up here?"

"I was given a choice. Come to New York and be a liaison to this rough-around-the-edges team I had experience with or resign. The only condition imposed was Morgan was the new district attorney assigned to all our cases. They said it was to ensure transparency in the bureau and beyond. I didn't hesitate. I picked up my kids and left. Got a quick and uncontested divorce before I stepped one inch out of the state."

"That explains why you're staying with your parents."

"You should know it takes a village to raise a child. With our hours and demands, it takes as many willing human beings as possible." She exhales, takes another sip of water, and hands me the bottle back. "His parents are suing me for grandparents' rights or full custody."

"What?"

"That's why I've been on edge. Simon? I can process it and deal with it in therapy. I've been given a new slate here, but his parents keep pulling me back. They've demanded I move back to Washington and allow them access to my kids. If nothing else, they expect me to put them on a plane to spend summers out there. My lawyer inquired about things, and it turns out they are hellbent on having the kids see their father yearly. It doesn't matter that they're in therapy and scarred from what Simon has done or that he signed over his parental rights. That man looked me in the eye and told me the boys were the best wingmen to attract a victim. He never loved our kids or me; we were simply a cover for him to hide behind."

The silence falls easily between the two of us. As I'm watching people come and go from the apartment building, the fire station blares, and firetrucks flood out of the station behind us.

"Sydney's a good kid," Karina says. "She's called me on a few things, and we've met for coffee. Smart detective, just trying to find her way."

"She never mentioned meeting you in person."

"Sworn to secrecy for obvious reasons. I didn't want you to know I was here. Not yet."

"You could have reached out."

"You had your drama going on. The Carnation Killer, not finding them in time to save that woman . . . It mustn't have been easy."

"I would have made time."

"I know, but I wasn't ready to face you yet either. I didn't know what you'd heard, read, or believed," Karina finishes. "Sydney was easy to talk to because we only talked shop."

"I don't think she's really happy running the tech department right now."

"You'd be surprised. She's been looking for her niche where she could contribute the most using all her degrees and experience. She loves the technological side, but she also loves being out in the field. Maybe she'll work with Logan when he comes back, be his eyes outside of the lab."

"You're optimistic."

"As long as there is breath, there is hope, Jasmine. My father taught me that."

Karina pulls her phone out, effectively shutting down the conversation. Hearing what she went through, the confirmation of all the reports, breaks my heart. It's one of those situations where you feel horrible for everything another human being has and continues to endure. Yet, regardless of all the negativity surrounding her, I'm thankful she is a part of our team. I wish it had been on her terms, her true choice, but like everything else in life, there's the path we want to follow, and the one destiny forces us to walk.

Chapter Ten

"I understand that, Morgan. I'm asking what you can do on your end." Karina's words force my eyes to open as the sun slowly illuminates the buildings around us. "Yes, his name is on that list, and no, I haven't approached him in a negative manner. We buzzed his apartment, and he wanted to discuss everything over the inter—" Karina rests her forehead in her hand, her thumb and index finger pressing into her scalp to alleviate the pressure. "No, I did not indulge him. Steele and I went back to our vehicle to wait him out."

I slowly realize where I am—a stakeout outside Barrett's house. Stretching forces a few pops along my spine and right shoulder as a yawn exits my mouth. Karina looks tired, her hair in disarray, the leather jacket long discarded. Her small notebook is littered with markings and doodles as she continues her phone conversation.

"Morgan, regardless of your concerns surrounding my abilities, your job is to assist this department. So, can you help us or not?" Karina says firmly, and I take that as my cue to stretch my legs.

I mindlessly reach for my cell phone in my jacket pocket. Feeling it empty, I look to the center console and see my phone on the floor next to the seat tracks. Sliding my hand down and grabbing it, I see I've got a ton of notifications, several missed calls— some from numbers I've never seen before—and a few text messages. Exiting the car, I shake my legs and walk to the small courtyard.

Where are you? Frankie sent at two in the morning. *Answer your phone!* She sent it again at three. Will sent several as well, all in a similar tone and wording. Frankie's last message causes my jaw to clench in pure emotion. *She's awake.* Sent at three thirty. My hands fumble with the phone, shaking as I try to dial my wife. The connection rings three times before I hear Will mumbling in the background.

"Frankie? Babe, can you hear me?" I hear Frankie talking, but everything is muffled as if she's covering the receiver.

"Honey, I can hear you. I was talking to Will."

"I'm sorry. I crashed in the car and my phone fell next to the center console. Hadley's awake? What do the doctors say? What's going on?"

"Sweetie, slow down. Yes, she was awake for a bit. As per your instructions, the doctors took her off the ventilator and said everything is headed in the right direction. She was in a lot of pain, so they administered something to help her rest. She'll be in and out for most of the day and maybe tomorrow. Considering her family and personal history, they don't want to use heavy drugs for more than a day. She asked about Logan."

"What'd you tell her?"

"That he's hanging on and that you went all 'protective older sister' on the doctors. She laughed before it caused some discomfort. I couldn't tell her the full truth. She has to get better first."

"Did they mention how long she might be in the hospital?"

"Jasmine, Hadley just woke up. Even if they were talking about releasing her from ICU, she'd move into the room next door. Will and the captain are discussing putting their beds in the same room. It might be an easier proposition to sell to the doctors since Hadley has been awake and responsive." I hear muffled voices in the background again, and I can hear Frankie answer, but it's not clear. "Chase is at school today and Mia is taking him for the weekend. I'll keep you posted on everything going on here. Just make sure your phone is on, charged, and not hidden in the crevices of your car, okay?"

The call disconnects before I can reply. I turn back to the vehicle; my pacing more than stretched my legs some time ago. Karina watches me carefully from the front of the SUV. Her phone put away, her arms are folded across her chest as she rests on the bumper.

"Everything okay?"

"So far. Hadley's off life support and woke up briefly." I stare at my cell phone as if it could magically transport me away from here and to the hospital.

"That's great news, and yet you seem like someone kicked your dog."

"It's stupid."

"Just spill it."

"It's Frankie. She never hangs up before saying 'I love you.'"

"Considering the circumstances and her location, I think she deserves a pass this one time."

"Yeah, I know. It's just out of the ordinary," I say, putting my phone securely away in its belt holster. "Considering our conversation yesterday, we good?"

"I . . ." Karina pauses. "I can't promise I won't be clipped when Morgan is around or when she's trying to extort information out of my team. I do feel better knowing we're on the same page and you know everything. I appreciate you listening and not . . ."

"Judging you? Declaring you a traitor to the force and a blight on the sanctity of the badge?" The sarcasm flies out of my mouth with gusto. "All levels of defenders have had stains on their shields worse than this. The military hides rapists, police hide racists, and the FBI . . . they hide the sticks that puncture rectums of the higher-ups."

Karina snickers at my comment. "Point is, you're no better or worse than anyone else. You didn't know. Just don't be an asshole," I finish before turning my attention back to the case. "Now, what did Morgan say? She going to assist or throw us into the deep end and pray we can swim?"

"While I love that imagery, no, she's not going to let us drown. Since Barrett was on our list of suspects and Sydney connected his IP address to specific posts and times, she's getting us a warrant for his computer. It's the best she can do for now."

"Is it specific to certain items within the computer, or do we have the latitude to look at anything installed? Search history . . ."

"My impression is the laptop and all its contents are included in the warrant." Karina pauses, looking up at the apartment complex. "We'll have to talk our way into his apartment, but then we'll have access to anything in plain sight."

"That's if he lets us in. He could easily hand us the laptop and slam the door. That doesn't cover the issue of multiple computers either."

"One battle at a time. Right now, Morgan's headed to the judge's chambers. She should be here in ten to twenty minutes." Karina looks at her watch. "Or sooner. Our call ended a while ago."

"While I'm sure she's expeditious, I doubt she will be here in ten minutes. I'd lean toward thirty or so."

"Trust me, Steele, she can, and she does." Karina looks over to the building. "He stayed inside all night. I hoped he would go out for dinner or something."

"Did Sydney find out where he worked?"

"Yeah." She scrolls through a few screens on her phone. "He works as a security guard at some warehouse in Midtown. Makes a decent living, no financial flags or significant debts."

"How does he afford an apartment on the Upper West Side of Manhattan on that salary?"

"Rent controlled lease transferred to him when his mother died. Sydney said he has a good-sized bank account, but the majority of the money came from his family and ex-wife."

"Who is she?"

"Amelia Barrett works down in the financial district. They met at Baruch and were married before they graduated. She's been stable financially and has job security. His employment history looks like a rap sheet for incompetence."

"Her career rose while his slowly tanked?"

"Gary was fired from half of the positions and resigned from the rest. He's maintained this current one for two years. Based on everything listed here, that seems like a personal best."

"Anything else?"

"Beyond the tirades online, not really. His digital signature is minimal, and we haven't had a chance to talk to his ex-wife yet. We need to look around his place and question him as best we can, given the circumstances."

"What about his cell? What if he keeps everything on there?"

"Statistically, doubtful. Predators don't carry their crimes with them. Makes them too vulnerable. Just like Simon, they save it in a place for reverence and reflection. Having it in something that could be hacked or just lost is not normal."

"True, but there are exceptions to the rule. If one is more on the voyeuristic side of things, they may carry everything with them."

"Still doubtful. It's not like having sex in public or watching two people do it. Carrying around the evidence would be like Jeffrey Dahmer walking around with fingers on toothpicks for snacks. They might want attention, but not like that."

"Okay, really disgusting image, but I get your point. If we can't prove Barrett was behind hurting Hadley and Logan, we're back to square one."

"Possibly, but we might find evidence of other crimes. His forum posts do reference some pornography; if he distributed it, we could arrest him. It would be much easier to prove, but the sentencing would be dependent on the extent of the crime. If it's federal, it'd be worse. Local, that's up to Morgan. She might plead him out to get bigger fish. He could be out before you know it."

Metal tapping on the driver's glass window forces a jump scare out of me usually only horror films succeed in eliciting. Morgan stands there, her rings resting against the glass. A single piece of paper held in her hands.

"Let's not get ahead of ourselves, dears." She turns to the apartment building. "Do you need an invitation, or are you coming?" Her heeled boots, dark-blue jeans, and suit jacket is completely different from her power persona attire from yesterday. Karina and I silently follow her through the parking lot to the lobby.

Morgan pushes a button repeatedly, holding it for three seconds or more. She ignores the voice trying to pop through the intercom and continues to press it. An older gentleman pushes through the stair entrance and over to us. He shakes his head, opening up the two locked doors in front of us.

"What do you want?"

"You're the building manager, yes?" Morgan asks smoothly.

"If you had given me a chance to reply, you would know that already."

"Excellent. We have a warrant for one of your tenants. We need access."

"Did you buzz the apartment?"

"Sir, I don't think you understand. We are serving a legal document to an individual who lives here. If we buzz him, as you so politely recommended, he could destroy evidence or run down the emergency exit while we're heading up the elevator. So, I suggest you allow us into the building to prevent all of that from happening."

The man says nothing as he slides to the side of the entryway. Morgan smiles as she heads to the elevator.

"Just wait here. We'll be back shortly," Morgan says as she passes the building manager.

"You didn't have to come along to execute the warrant," Karina says. I begin silently praying to anyone listening that this doesn't turn into a battle between them. "We don't know what he's capable of, and it could go south."

"While I appreciate your concern, I wanted to handle this personally. You two will be doing all the work; I will simply be witnessing the interaction."

"And reporting back?" I utter before my brain can shut me up.

"Yes, I will. Do you have a problem with that?" She turns to Karina and me, waiting for an argument. Finding none, she turns back to the elevator doors. "It also allows me to observe the scene and his behavior. Three heads are better than two overtired, dreadfully dressed ones."

The doors open, and she walks out and to the left, following the signs to the upper alphabet apartments. Karina looks up and down at both of our wrinkled, slept-in-a-car outfits.

"She's got a point," I say. In response, Karina makes a grunting noise that sounds like a whale crying for help.

Morgan pushes the button for 16F before Karina and I reach the door. She presses it again when we reach her side. Stepping out of the way, she hands Karina the search warrant and waits.

"What do you want?" The voice comes through the door. I'm sure his eye is glued to the small peephole.

"Mr. Gary Barrett?"

"Yeah, who wants to know?"

"Agent Marlow. We spoke yesterday over the intercom."

"I told you I don't have to speak to you. Get out of my building!"

"Sir, as we previously discussed, we returned with a warrant."

The door opens slightly, blocked by the chain latch. A white hand with thick black hair on the knuckles and hard callouses slides out ever so slightly. "Give it to me."

Karina looks over to Morgan, who nods before she hands it to him. The hand quickly retracts, and the door slams shut. I count the seconds of silence in my head. One Mississippi, two Mississippi, three Mississippi . . . "If he refuses to answer, we'll need the building manager," I tell them, wondering why we didn't bring him in the first place.

Morgan waves off my concern. "If necessary, I'll go get him."

The sound of the chain sliding across the channel grabs my attention. The door opens, revealing a tall man of average build with a full head of brown hair streaked with some gray. He steps to the side so the three of us can enter without a fight. I'm instantly on edge. Considering how much he argued yesterday, the lack of argument now gives me pause.

The short hallway opens into a nice-sized living space. There's a small kitchen to my right, with a table and chair along the wall next to it. A couch and massive television rest near the large windows overlooking the city. The sparsely decorated apartment looks void of everything from emotion to a personal touch. It's as if this is a place one sleeps more than lives. Unlike other suspects' places that are meticulously cleaned or decorated deliberately, this is just empty.

Karina pulls an evidence bag and latex gloves out of her jacket pocket and turns to Barrett. "Desktop? Laptop?"

"Laptop," he says, playing with his hands in front of his chest.

"And where is it?" Karina follows up as the man is slow to move.

"Bedroom on the nightstand." Karina walks past him and into the other room.

"What are you looking for?" he asks me as my eyes continue to search the place.

"I like what you've done with the place." My gaze falls to a small shelving unit next to the couch. New York Mets items fill it: some old beer bottles with logos, several bobbleheads, and on top, a glass tank filled with baseballs, including one from the 2000 World Series that appears to be signed by Mike Piazza.

"This is worth a ton of money," I say. "You go to the game?"

"Game four at Shea. I went with my wife . . . well, then-girlfriend."

"My mom took me; second to last row. She kept yelling at the place to be quiet 'cause she had a migraine."

"Amelia, my ex-wife, wasn't a fan either. She was bored, and the people near us were all Yankee fans. I managed to grab a ball, but the autograph came much later at an event." He pulls his arms behind his back as he rocks from heel to toe.

Karina comes out of the bedroom, holding the laptop in the evidence bag. "Would you like to come down to the station with us, Mr. Barrett?"

"Am I under arrest for something?"

"No sir," I answer, pulling a card out of my wallet. "But this is an active investigation, and we could use your help. If you could please come to the station to answer a few questions, it would be greatly appreciated."

He takes my card but manages to hold my hand weirdly. His finger grazes over my thumb. The small smirk and glimmer in his eyes show a different side to the nervous person we first encountered. It also makes the hairs on the back of my neck stand on edge.

"I'll be down there in a few hours. Give you time to search through my stuff." He leans forward, inches away from my face, as the words and his need for a mint hits my face.

"Steele," Karina calls me from the doorway, and I gently push past Barrett to leave.

The door closes behind us, and we leave the apartment without a confrontation.

"Anyone else find that odd?" I ask the other two women with me.

"I've never served a warrant when the person on the receiving end was calm," Karina adds.

"Feel like talking to the ex? See if that's part of his personality or if it's out of character?"

"He read it beforehand. Knew what we wanted. He's a cunning piece of work. I also dare say he's your guy," Morgan finishes as the elevator opens. She casually walks back inside, hits the lobby button, and turns to the two of us. "What? I've seen criminals like him before. Now get in here; let's get the laptop down to Sydney before the two of your heads explode."

***

Logan's office, now occupied by Sydney Locke, has gone from fanboy clean to messy confusion. The wall of screens behind her shows various frames and calculations for comparing specific parameters. Each screen flashes from one frame, then lines, dots, and more appear; measurements are made before a new one appears.

"Here you go, Sydney, straight out of Gary Barrett's house."

Sydney grabs the evidence bag housing the laptop and places it to the side of the desk. Her eyes look tired, red, and blotchy like she's been up all night.

"I've been going over all the statistics, and I can confidently say the person in all three locations is the same one. The physical attributes are almost identical, as is the cadence and usage of his right hand to talk on the phone. Facial recognition software is spotty due to the hat he always has on. Plus, it's like he knows the camera system." She rambles as she grabs the energy drink next to her. It's then I notice the line of empty cans on the desk. She has been up all night and is now running on pure adrenaline, sugar, and caffeine. She needs a nap.

"Or he was busy looking at his phone at every intersection. At this point, everyone does that. I don't know if I would quantify that as intelligence or idiocy." Karina points to the screens showing the suspect's head down.

"Why wear the same hat with the same logo? How common is it?" I ask, cutting in.

"That's where it gets really interesting." She clicks on the keyboard, her nails tapping away. Three images come up right next to each other, all zoomed in on the trucker hat reading *OUTLAW WOMEN*. The two words rest in a block formation over a symbol of a military-looking knife. "That hat was only given to members of the cast and crew from a little indie film shot in 2009. It made it to a few festivals but went nowhere beyond that. The film won several awards and was a cult hit, but the producers refused to release it or try to get a distribution deal. According to interviews with some of the bigger names, the contracts seemed too good to be true, with higher than normal percentages of profits and payments as deferment."

"Sydney, while I'm sure this is fascinating information, how does this connect to our case?"

"Well, that little film was the first major role for a young up-and-coming actress whose previous credits included only a Pantene commercial." Sydney pulls up a picture of Hadley wearing her *Outlaw Women* hat, arms outstretched and smiling.

"Okay, so now we have a connection between the two but not necessarily between the crimes."

"Karina, it's enough to get the guy down here for questioning," Sydney continues, her hand shaking from all the chemicals coursing through her system.

"He's already coming."

"True, but he thinks we're going to grill him about his laptop, not his connection to Had," I add.

"I want printouts of every image you have of him from each location. I want you to start searching his laptop and find out whatever you can." Karina's phone goes off, and she walks out of the room without saying another word.

"She still being difficult?" Sydney asks.

"Nah, it's all sorted." I look up at the screens and back down at Sydney. "You need a break. Is there anything I can help you with?"

"I've got the team running through all the possible links between Hadley and Barrett beyond the film. If you want to comb through his extended file, go for it. I've compiled everything from nursery school to now. It's a ton of shit and most of it will be useless, but it's worth a shot."

"I'll do it if you crash out on the couch for half an hour. You need a power nap before you have a heart attack from all those energy drinks."

"I couldn't . . ."

"Sydney, you'll miss something if you're not rested." I pull up a chair next to Logan's desk and take over her reading. She plugs the computer into our system, clicks some keys, and it boots up. She yawns as I look at the three-hundred-page file she's put together.

"Please tell me this has some pictures?"

"Yeah, a few. Not many. You're a trained detective, Steele. You know how to skim, right?" She laughs as my eyes start scrolling through mind-numbing information. Sydney starts to run a scan before she lies down on the couch. She's out when I look up to ask her a question. It's time-sensitive stuff, but she's not used to any of us like this. I lean back in the chair, put my boots on the desk, and settle in to read.

Gary Barrett, born to Winifred and Emmanuel Barrett. Grew up in Alphabet City with his older brother Gregory. Father worked for IBM and mother was a homemaker. They attended temple consistently, obeyed the Sabbath, and were prominent in the community. Family photos attached to some newspaper article show a normal and happy family.

Both boys attended a private nursery school. No record of any issues during those years. Both boys attended local public school for elementary. They were above-average students, and Gregory proved to be quite athletic. No issues, and they were exemplary kids.

The monotony of this information increases as the same "perfect children" story continues to emerge. It's the same crap that's spewed everywhere. The teachers write report cards and give information the parents want to hear so they can keep their jobs. In every case I've ever worked, there has never been a pile of papers about a troubled child from a teacher. School psychologist, sure. Educators, never. They have so many chairs to worry about daily that it's simpler to have canned answers for these forms than to truly fill them out. Besides, their bosses and some parents would have their heads for labeling a child as anything other than wonderful.

Throughout their entire educational career, both boys seem destined to be successful. Gregory graduated from MIT and headed to Silicon Valley for work. He still works out there and has his name attached to several technological developments that are well above my head in technobabble.

Gary, on the other hand, went into finance. In college, he had an internship with Morgan Stanley for a semester. I assume he wasn't offered a job there, because when he graduated, he worked for J.P. Morgan Chase. That seems to be his longest tenure overall, lasting for just over two years. He was married to Amelia during this time and lived down in the Battery Park area.

Around his thirtieth birthday, things change direction. He was fired from his job. The attached explanation is redacted heavily. The years tick by with various hirings and firings in his file. He began working freelance crew jobs as a production assistant on low-budget films. The next few pages involve his divorce. He cites irreconcilable differences, but her filing is very different. She discusses the theft of assets and an affair. The date of the filing is December 2009. That's the same year Hadley's film completed principal photography.

Hadley would have told me if she was involved with this guy at any point in her career. The defense would use her normal kindness as flirtation. It was always a problem and something she worked on daily to tone down. People interpret her willingness to be polite or compassionate as desire and lust. That was never the case. Hadley would never break up a marriage. She always told me her pain she could handle, but causing someone else pain because of her behavior would eat her alive for the rest of her life.

The question about the affair still lingers in my mind. If he was attracted to Hadley and obsessed with her, he could have been having an emotional affair. In his mind, he might have even been having a physical one as well. No matter what, this adds more circumstantial evidence to the pile, none of which is a slam dunk for the attempted murder charges. I need more. And fast.

It's been an hour. Time to wake Sydney up and go to work.

Chapter Eleven

The streetlights click on one by one as the shadows of tall skyscrapers crawl along the pavement, obscuring the natural light. Reporters have come and gone as they usually do with all the typical questions about the shooting: "What laws are in place to protect citizens?" or "How far do they actually reach?" The faux outrage at the distinct lack of privacy for individuals, mainly women, forces me out of the press room and outside. The carbon monoxide-filled air is much cleaner than the shit those fiends are slinging in the conference room.

If we all had privacy, those gossip and paparazzi-filled rags would be at the bottom of every birdcage in the city. Instead, they sell like wildfire, preying on those who are making good money doing what they love but paying the price for it. There's a lack of compassion as it trickles down to those with no money or power. The poor women who go to work every day and have an ex-boyfriend that doesn't understand the word goodbye. That kind of a "lack of power."

Instead of thinking about compassion or positivity, they feed the monster of envy. Showing all those who have "something" as deserving of our intrusion. The populace feasts on it, while corporations slowly remove all their freedoms with every app they download onto a device. It's maddening that no one thinks about anything beyond themselves. The more I work in this field and the more I read, the less of humanity I understand.

"Jazz?" Victor walks out the front doors, his tie slightly askew. "What are you doing out here?"

"Fresh air."

"We're not by the water or on the roof. The only air you're getting is comprised of microscopic particles slowly killing your alveoli," he says sarcastically, leaning on the railing next to me. "Seriously, what's on your mind?"

"I haven't seen you lately. How are you holding up?" I divert the conversation to something more appropriate.

"Managing. I've been in touch with Frankie. I know how you prefer to discuss other things until you feel comfortable sharing your emotions."

"You sound like a bad episode of Dr. Phil." I laugh a little.

"He's not a real doctor, so I don't see the reference. Plus, have you seen that man dress? Lord, does he need a stylist." Victor looks out into the sea of vehicles on the road. "It's okay if you're not ready. Just know we're here."

"It's not about being anything right now, Vic. I keep tracking down these flimsy leads but come up short. Like I'm trying to hold onto a fistful of sand, but it keeps getting smaller. I'm only human, and I'd like some modicum of control over something right now." The words drain my energy as my body presses deeper into the railing. "God, I hate this place."

"I've been sidelined with numerous court cases, paperwork that would make any of you cry, and finding an apartment that won't bankrupt Lil and me. Yet, I'm standing here with living patients that make my skin crawl. Life has a way of throwing curveballs at you when you think you're getting a fastball right down the middle. I get it."

"A baseball reference from the man who hates dirt?" The sincere laugh bubbles up before I can control it. The man that would bellow if the table at a bar was sticky is referencing sports. The world has teetered on its head. "And moving in together already?"

"Well, Lillian is a die-hard Mets fan. I don't understand why they always lose. Secondly, Lil and I . . . we seem to fit, and it feels right." Victor takes a very deep breath and exhales slowly. I can tell the conversation is turning back to the reality of our situation. "I looked over her medical file. If the bullet had been a few inches . . ." He falters, and I look up to see him struggling to hold his composure. "It was like Garrison all over again. Watching you leave us, praying for a miracle. You both were lucky, and eventually that luck runs out. I've seen firsthand what one simple bullet can do to a family. I've seen people collapse on the other side of the glass. I don't want to be one of them, so let me help."

"Vic, you're here doing exactly what we need. But without a body . . ."

"I'm more than the goddamned coroner, and you know it!" His voice rises in frustration.

I stand up and place my hands on his shoulders. "I know you want to do more; we all do. Right now, being here is what we need." I pull him into a hug and feel his arms pull me tighter.

"I don't want you to think any of us are slacking."

"It never crossed my mind." I pause and pull back a bit. "Lil's been buried. Maybe she could use another set of hands?"

"Steele, you ready?" Karina calls out as she exits the door toward the row of police vehicles parked out front. "We got an interview."

I kiss Victor on the top of his head before hugging him one more time. This entire case has been filled with violence but also monotony—interviews, waiting for evidence, and praying for some connection. While a good crime scene offers some hope, this ground game only offers me step goals. I think that's something to scare my new therapist with later this week.

***

The moonlight reflects off the glass windows of the Goldman Sachs building in lower Manhattan. Lights pockmark the exterior as employees continue to work into the evening hours. Unlike the rest of the city, the financial district slows down with the end of the business day. Even with the few still working, people still wander about, seeing the 9/11 memorial or taking photos of Alexander Hamilton's grave at Trinity Church. It's peaceful.

The almost deserted lobby of this gargantuan complex has ostenta-tious art pieces hanging from the ceiling. Computerized turnstiles pre-vent those of us without a pass or computer chip under our skin from getting in. A small, white laminate counter sits to the left where a portly security guard watches us intently.

"They have their own damn Shake Shack outside the building. This is the perfect example of money and control to excess. Do they have people cleaning gold toilets or, better yet, wiping the CEO's ass for them?" My whispered words cause Karina to fight back a smile.

"Can I help you ladies?" the man says through a long yawn.

"We're here to see Amelia Barrett please," Karina says while I continue taking in the sheer height of the lobby ceilings and expensive artwork.

The security guard leans back and uses his index fingers to bang on the keyboard in front of him. "Two t's?" he asks.

"Two r's and two t's, yes," Karina answers as he hits backspace and starts again.

"Technology. The more it advances, the more we need a sledgeham-mer," I say, trying to lighten up the situation. It falls flat.

"There's no Amelia Barrett here, ma'am." His words ring curiously in my ears.

"She might be going by her maiden name." Karina opens up her phone and scrolls frantically through some files. "Tovar. Amelia Tovar. T as in Tango, O as in Oscar, V as in Victor, A as in Alpha and R as in Romeo." The guard plugs away at the keyboard again. He stops and squints at something on the screen.

"And who are you??"

"Agent Karina Marlow of the FBI and Detective Jasmine Steele from the NYPD."

The security guard picks up the phone and squints at the screen again as he dials. He turns to face us, his eyes boring holes through my face as the phone rings. The skeptical expression remains as we hear muffled sounds on the other end as he grunts his replies. Hanging up the phone, he reaches for two stickers and places them on the countertop.

"Sign in on the tablet and show me your identification." The two of us hand over our credentials as Karina writes our names on the tablet with her finger. He puts my badge up against his face as if sniffing it will make it more real. He turns his head and does the same thing to Karina's before handing them back. I wish I carried disinfecting wipes.

"Thirtieth floor; her assistant will meet you by the elevator." He hands us the two visitor stickers with today's date written on it. "Bring these back before you leave."

The two of us walk away and head up into the heights of hell. The elevator LCD screens flash floor numbers as we speed up the floors far too fast for my stomach. The boxcar slows as we approach the thirtieth floor, and luckily, I haven't painted the carpet a new color. The robotic voice reads out the number as the doors gracefully slide open. A young Asian woman wearing heels, pinstripe pants, and matching vest with a white shirt, her hair up in a bun, waits for us.

"Detective Steele, Agent Marlow?" Her words are clipped, very businesslike.

"Yes," we say in unison like trained seals.

"With me, please."

She turns and walks away without waiting for our reply. Her steps are measured, like a perfect iambic pentameter poem. Her hands remain clasped behind her as she turns the corner and stops in front of a massive door. She knocks, and a muffled voice says something I can't understand. Our guide pushes the door open and remains in the doorway.

"Can I get you anything? Coffee? Water?" she asks us.

"Nothing, thank you," I answer. Karina is looking out the window at the waterfront view and says nothing.

The woman nods and closes the door behind her. Amelia Tovar is pacing, and she holds one finger up to the two of us and continues her conversation on the phone. I took Mandarin in college as an undergrad requirement. I know nothing but the sounds and curses, but Amelia's accent is almost perfect. Her wrist has a small tattoo on her light brown skin that is only visible when her watch moves down her forearm. Her dark black curls bounce with every runway step. Her impeccable look and posture at this late hour astound me. In her line of work, most people would have kicked those heels across the room by now. She ends her call and walks up to Karina first.

"Amelia Tovar," she says to Karina. "You are?"

"Agent Karina Marlow, and this is my partner Detective Jasmine Steele." The two shake hands before Karina leads her over to me.

"Pleasure to meet you." Amelia's hazel eyes focus on me for longer than I'm comfortable. She smirks and sits behind her desk. She motions for us to sit, and we do.

"I didn't think the FBI was interested until we dealt with the SEC."

"We don't have anything to do with any white-collar investigation. We're here about your ex-husband, Gary Barrett."

Her entire body tenses at those words. Her right thumb slides across her left palm, digging the nail in on every pass. Her chair creaks as she leans back, and her legs cross, but the scratching continues. Her ex-husband is a trigger, but why?

"I'm sorry, detective. I haven't spoken to him since we finalized our divorce. I don't know what else I can tell you. I'm also not comfortable getting involved in an investigation of my ex," she answers softly, trying to shut the conversation down right away.

"I understand that, ma'am, but we were hoping you could help us." Karina leans forward in the chair next to me.

"Please, call me Amelia." The woman uncrosses her legs and leans her elbows on the thick mahogany desk as her thumb never ceases its assault. "I divorced him, wiped him from my life and my name. Kept my nose clean and worked my way up to the top." Her voice wavers with a tinge of anger.

"May I ask what your title is?" I ask.

"I'm the Executive Director and Vice President of Investment Management Internal Audit."

"And what does a person of your level do exactly?" The follow-up question is out of my mouth before Karina can interject.

"I don't see how it's relevant, but I am the one who verifies that everything within these walls is 'up to snuff' shall we say. Now what has that little . . .What has Gary done now?"

"He's currently under investigation due to his connection with a porn distribution ring."

"He wouldn't distribute," she says matter-of-factly. "He'd download it, use it to . . . help us in the bedroom, and that's it. He's too embarrassed to share it, let alone admit he needed it."

"While I appreciate the candidness, his name came up, so we are required to look into it," Karina begins. "When you were married, did Mr. Barrett show signs of aggressive behavior?"

"He broke the Keurig because the cups we bought were for the wrong machine," she says, laughing at the memory. "Truthfully, I don't think aggressive and Gary go in the same sentence."

"You said he broke the coffee machine; did he show other signs of violence?" Karina continues her line of questioning.

"You misunderstand. We bought the wrong reusable cup and it got stuck. Gary was struggling to get the stupid thing out of the container. He was forceful because he was frustrated with the stupid thing. Add that to his clumsiness, and it was bound to be destroyed. The man was smart as hell, but hand him a screwdriver and you'd think he was a Neanderthal," Amelia says, leaning back once again. Her thumb is no longer digging into her other palm. Instead, it's pressing deeply into her elbow as her arms are crossed in front of her.

"I appreciate the clarification, but I would like to know if Mr. Barrett was ever violent to you or others around you," Karina presses.

"You're serious." Amelia shakes her head and focuses on something behind us. "Gary was too afraid to hit another human being. When we were dating, men would come up to me during our dates and Gary would cower. I had to stand up for myself." She pauses, her eyes coming to rest back on Karina. "It should have been a red flag, but instead, it made me love him more. He didn't believe in outward violence."

"What did he believe in?" I ask quickly.

"People think wars are waged with guns and bombs, but the real war is all in cyberspace. Gary knew it." She stops, turns her attention to Karina, and opens her mouth to speak but closes it right away. I can see her struggling with how to express what's floating around in her mind. "I had a boss when I was working retail to pay for school. Gary and I had just started dating at the time, and he was very supportive. My boss was a sexist piece of work and asked me on a date. I politely refused because of several reasons. One day he cornered me, and as I felt the metal rack dig into my back, he told me he was done being nice, and I was expected to go on a date with him like a good woman. I refused again and, with Gary's help, reported him anonymously to my superiors. Long story short, my boss found out, the company denied everything, and I was fired. Two days later, video of my boss ranting on video about women was all over social media."

"And you think Gary was responsible?" Karina continues.

"He always denied it, but I watched him search everywhere for information on the guy. Kept asking me random questions so he could hone in. It wasn't just the video, but bank accounts, arrest records—Gary manipulated it all. That's why I know he's not a physically violent man. He's passive-aggressive. And yes, I married him knowing this. We're all entitled to our mistakes."

"You two attended Baruch College together, is that correct?" Karina changes directions.

"Yes," she answers firmly, leaving no room for discussion.

"How was he as a student?"

"You could easily subpoena his transcripts. I don't understand why you need me—"

"It's not so much the grades as it is his state of mind. We're trying to figure out what kind of person he was at varying points." I try to smooth things over and relieve the tension. "Tell us only what you feel comfortable sharing about those college years. Did anything stand out?"

She takes a sip from the metal water bottle on the corner of her desk. Her thumb is back to digging holes in her hand, and her eyes stare off into space.

"He was so smart but never finished anything on time without me prodding him constantly. He'd read a textbook once and remember it verbatim. I never understood why he couldn't just apply that ability to anything in the real world."

"In your divorce filings, you mentioned theft and an affair. Do you feel comfortable going into more detail?"

"Do I feel comfortable? Rehashing painful old memories is not my idea of comfortable, but I don't have much choice here. Gary was a good man, compassionate even, but not if you were his family. He was never there, always helping everyone else and ignoring the one who was right in front of him. He made managers and CEOs love him. He was promised partnerships if he just kept his head down and kept working hard. He was the apple of the office's eye. I'd come home, and dishes were always in the sink, clothes sitting in the hamper, and he'd be on the couch watching television. Weekends, he'd sit and watch his horror film collection. If I worked late, I'd come home and he'd want to know what was for dinner. There was never any consideration of our life together."

"These horror movies, any specific ones?" I immediately jump in with the follow-up question.

"Any with actresses with big tits, blonde hair, and blood." She laughs, leaning back in her chair as a memory flashes across her mind. "Would you believe he walked away from his six-figure salary to be a production assistant on some low-budget film? He never discussed any of this with me. Just up and walks away. I told him to go to school and learn all about film; I'd support him. I wanted him to be happy doing what he wanted to do."

"How was your relationship after he changed careers?" I ask, knowing full well Hadley was working on that film.

"Bad to worse. He checked out. What little intimacy we had dwindled to nothing. He was a totally different man. He wasn't even fazed when I kicked him out." She leans back once again and takes a few seconds to collect her thoughts. "Gary is a good man when he's your friend or a colleague. Once you go past that line in the sand, he's not the same. That doesn't make him evil. It makes him . . . pathetic."

"The theft?"

"He had closed our joint bank accounts and spent the money without my knowledge. He returned it within a month or so of signing the papers, so I dropped it."

"Did Mr. Barrett ever exhibit obsessive tendencies during your marriage?"

"That's an odd question, Agent Marlow. He was always into reading his books and watching horror films, but I don't know if that would qualify as an obsession. It felt more like my marriage falling apart."

"Do you know this woman?" I place my cell phone on the desk, showing Hadley's headshot.

"Oh yes, she was his favorite little horror *babe*." Amelia holds the phone, her eyes transfixed. They slowly widen and, for the first time, discomfort and fear show in them. "She's the actress . . ." Amelia drops my phone on the desk, stands, and walks over to the window. One hand loosely covers her mouth and the other is pressed against the small of her back. "She's the actress from the news . . . the one at Chelsea Piers."

Amelia turns to face the two of us, her arms shaking as she wraps them around her body. "She was shot."

"Yes, she was."

"You think he . . .he's not a violent man." Her sentences fragment and her eyes move around as if trying to make sense of the situation. "He never raised a hand to me at all."

"Amelia," Karina says and stands up to face the woman. "We don't know what happened. We're doing our jobs, and it led us here. You say he's not capable of physically harming anyone, but could he have been pushed over the edge?"

"I don't think so, but . . ."

"But what?" Karina presses. "Please, we need to know."

"He lashed out at his mother when she pushed him too far. She nagged him for something, I don't remember what now, but he was so mad he finally screamed at her. He said horrible things because that's what you do when you're angry. He's normally not that kind of guy, though. It still felt very out of character for him. Just like the fucking coffee machine, it's a specific incident, not Gary himself."

"Did he assault her?" I try to keep Amelia on a train of thought through her shock.

"What?" She stops, her hands clamping onto her biceps hard.

"During this argument was Gary physical?"

"No, we just came home, complaining the whole subway ride. I went to bed, and he stayed up fuming. He was always meticulous, a planner. That's one of the things that made me fall in love with him at first, you know? He wouldn't react right away. He'd think about what happened for a long time. He called it his 'processing executable file.' Then he would make a plan for how to fix the issue. He never stayed angry for very long. He was rational."

She finished sounding more like she was pleading for us to understand than anything else. "I think I'd like you to leave now," she says abruptly.

I can see all the walls closing in around her and the realization that she might have been married to a monster. Everything in her body language screams flight, and I can tell her cutting us off is her way of fleeing the stress of the conversation. If we're not here, she can ignore it or pretend she never knew. Ignorance is bliss.

"Amelia . . ." Karina tries to calm her.

"No, I think I've talked enough already. Please leave."

Without saying a word, the two of us leave and find our way out of the building.

***

As we pull up to the warehouse, it seems alive with activity inside, unlike the downtown offices. The tall building has a storefront and a garage entrance to the left of a small doorway. The joys of Manhattan property is having everything crammed into one small block.

"You call ahead?" Karina asks as we walk to the glass door.

"Do we ever?" I answer sarcastically. "If he's on shift, we don't want him to run, and if he's not, we don't want someone to tip him off."

"He already knows, Steele. We were at his place. If he's half as smart as Amelia alluded to, he knows."

"He knows we're searching his shit, but even the smartest guys out there forget we cover the ground game as well."

Karina ignores the conversation and pushes the button. I can hear her counting under her breath as the seconds tick away. She presses it again, holding the infernal thing down longer. The sound causes pain in my eardrums. A man in full security uniform purposefully trots down the stairs one at a time.

At the landing, he stares at the two of us, his shaved head and bulging muscles designed to intimidate us. My hand slides the edge of my coat jacket open, showing my gun, while my other hand holds my badge in his eyeline.

"What do you want?"

"I'm FBI Agent Marlow, and this is Detective Steele. We were hoping to talk and get a tour of the place. Nothing more," Karina answers.

"You got a warrant?"

"Have you done anything wrong?"

"Not the point," he answers dutifully. "I ain't incriminating myself."

"During our investigation, the name Gary Barrett was brought up. Since you're not him, talking to us won't hurt you."

The guard takes a few seconds to think it over. Then he unlocks the door.

"Come in and don't go up the stairs." He opens the door, and we stop on the small landing, pressed up against the wall so we don't get in his way. The guard closes the door and locks it. "Follow me, but stay close. I have rounds to do so you'll have to ask your questions as we walk. If I don't want to answer, I reserve the right to skip it. Name's Neil."

"Of course," Karina answers as we follow him up the stairs. "Do you have a last name?"

"Don't we all?"

"Not if you're Cher or Madonna or Beyoncé . . . " I try to lighten the mood, but Neil's nonplussed expression means I failed miserably. "Would you mind sharing your full name?"

"Yes, I would." Neil opens the door, and we enter a wide-open space with desks strategically placed in the center.

"I thought Mr. Barrett worked security for a warehouse."

"He does. This place is literally called The Warehouse."

"What does the company handle?"

"I don't ask. I just do my job and keep the place sealed up tight. No one in or out without the proper authority."

"Mr. Barrett, what shift does he usually work?"

"Days mostly; he covers a night shift once in a while," he spits out quickly.

"You don't seem too thrilled with that."

"Overnights pays more, but he's a trust fund baby who doesn't need to work or support his family. The rest of us have to deal with the bad shifts to survive."

"Does he ever exhibit any negative behaviors or outbursts?" I ask, and Neil stops walking for a second.

"Yeah, two weeks ago, he demanded to work my shift. I mean the guy's a fucking tool because he went to my boss instead of bringing it to me. I would have switched if he just gave me a good reason, but the guy doesn't say shit to me."

Karina and Neil continue to walk, but my feet remain firmly planted in front of a wall of printers. Specifically, 3D ones. A recycling container sits next to the unit. At the bottom of each one rests white, blue, and green blocks of plastic.

"Karina." I raise my voice, knowing the two are still taking steps away from me.

"What is it?"

"Who has access to these printers?" I ask Neil, hoping he can fill in the gaps but unsure if he is privy to this kind of information.

"When I work days, the doors are open and anyone can use it. One of the techs helped me make a racecar for my kid once. Really cool shit. Can we keep moving? Gotta finish my rounds."

I grab a quick picture on my cell before following them and continuing the path around the building. I tune out the conversation as I type out a message to Sydney. I know this is going to be a long night, but I think it's best if we try to cover as much as possible.

I need you to look up anything and everything to do with The Warehouse. I attach the photo and send it while the other two are busy a few steps ahead of me. Sydney replies with a few emojis that make no sense to me followed by a thumbs-up emoji, so I assume she's on it.

"We appreciate your time, and if you can think of anything that might help us with the investigation, please give me a call." I see Karina ending everything with her card and a handshake.

The two of us walk back to the car and into the noise of the busy city, even at this late hour. Karina flips through her notes as the locks on the doors snap shut behind us. Climbing into the driver's seat, I finally listen to the voicemail Frankie left me when I was downtown.

"Hey baby, things are stable here. Chase is refusing to leave his Aunt Hadley, so the doctors put a cot in her room. They're playing 500 Rummy right now, and Hadley's wiping the floor with our son. I think it's been good for both of them. Will, Captain Zeile, and I are working on a profile to see if your suspect fits. It's been difficult since we have to keep it from everyone around us." She takes a deep breath, and I swear I can hear her thinking. "Logan's numbers haven't changed in either direction. Not sure what it means beyond him being stable. I love you so much; please be careful no matter what you're doing, sweetheart. Call me later. Bye."

The voicemail ends, and I lower the phone to my lap. Karina continues to go through her notes as the pieces start falling into place in my mind. I'm sure if Karina and I were discussing the case right now, we'd both agree Gary is our main suspect and probably our perp. I think we've known that since we eliminated everyone else. It's the first time we know, almost exclusively, that he is the person to focus on. Just like Logan's lack of change, I don't know if that's a good or bad thing.

Chapter Twelve

S ydney dances around the office as she works, and her jovial mood lightens mine. Karina wanted to talk to her boys before coming inside, so I'm alone, leaning on the doorframe and watching my colleague with a smile. Her surprisingly beautiful voice fills the room, and I can see a few others looking our way.

"You going to an open mic night sometime?"

Sydney drops whatever she's holding and fumbles to mute the music from her laptop. Once it's off, she brushes down her clothing and fixes her hair. Considering how she's been around the team and me for some time, I'm surprised by the action.

"Next time, can you knock and give me a heads-up?"

"Sydney, it's me. Sing and dance away. In our line of work, you need to blow off steam. Some buy expensive shoes; others go to the range. I shoot zombies and laugh. We all deal with it in our own way."

"That might be true, but I'd still appreciate it if you knocked."

"Sure, I will make a conscious effort." I walk in and sit down in front of the desk. "Did you find anything?"

"Just the basics. The Warehouse's website has a bunch of long-winded mission statements, interviews, and press releases on it, but underneath it all, they are simply a technological company." Sydney looks down at her laptop and brings up the website on the screen behind her. "Nothing nefarious going on within their financials. They handle security protocols and have a small internal development team."

"So, they handle what . . . firewalls, malware blockers, and that kind of thing?"

"In a way, yes, but they also can fortify new designs and testing. The company is in the black as far as I can see. I sent the information up to forensic accounting, but I don't think they'll find anything there."

"Okay, but what does Barrett have to do with all of this? How does he fit in?"

"His best friend and former best man, Todd Hanson, is the CEO." Sydney brings up a photo of the two from Gary's wedding. "They attended college and were in the same fraternity. Our track record of friendships gone wrong continues."

"Did Todd do anything illegal or just give his friend the job?"

"I couldn't find out much, but again, it seems like it was all aboveboard."

"Okay, so he just so happens to get a job at his friend's place that just so happens to have 3D printers?"

"That would be part of the testing and development. They can create the item on a much smaller scale to see how truly functional it may or may not be. The software side is more lucrative and probably pays all their bills, but the rest can give them residuals on the back end of a project. It's a genius two-pronged approach to the company's stability in a really difficult field."

"Yeah, that was a lot of information that remains over my level of understanding at this point. What did you find on the laptop?"

"I sent over a file to Morgan with all the pertinent information," Sydney says as Karina walks back into the office in a huff.

"You did what?" Karina barks as she enters the room.

"She did her job," I defend in a calm tone. "Sydney wouldn't have known, Karina. She was just doing what she thought was right."

"Right . . . What did you send her?"

Sydney sits down and attacks her computer again. The screen shows the desktop and a few file folders that seem rather suspicious in title alone.

"He's got a lot of random photos from all of Hadley's films. Including *Outlaw Queen*, he has photos of the two of them as well a video or two of her talking to him. Normal fan stuff."

"Barrett was really into Hadley, we knew that, and now it's been reinforced from two sources. I'm more concerned about how deep his obsession with her goes. How has he managed to keep tabs on everything she's doing? Has he followed her and Logan? There are more questions than answers here," I say.

"He put a ton of security encryptions on here. We've only managed to access two file folders that were buried under several layers of different ciphers. It took a while, but we're hoping the rest of the files are under the same keys. Hopefully, he hid something more interesting in the remaining five folders, but there's no guarantee."

Several windows pop across the screen, including one for 3D printing of various items from knives to guns. They're detailed in their descriptions, blueprint specifications, and practical usages. The YouTube saved search shows a myriad of videos of individuals using the printed weapons, including some being fired. They show how to create, use, and dispose of these weapons. It's an assassin's handbook available to anyone with access to the internet.

"How difficult was this to crack?"

"More tedious than I would have liked. His cipher was annoying to figure out as well. It turns out it was based on the rules of a horror film. Barrett's smart and devious as hell, but he's up against one of the best teams in the state. We'll decode these last files or die trying . . ." She cringes as the last words fall from her mouth. "Sorry, poor choice of words,"

"It's fine." I shrug it off, trying not to think of the reality surrounding her phrasing. "You sent this to Morgan?"

"Along with this." Sydney opens another file folder. Images of women in various poses and stages of undress fill the large screen behind her. Several of their faces show looks of utter terror as they're covered in blood or being held in torturous positions. A few women lie on their backs, tears on their cheeks as they fight a hand grasped tightly around their throat. The pictures continue to scroll across the screen, each more horrific than the one before it.

"Is there a way to tell which are screen captures and which are real?" The horror in front of me reminds me of my youth, the photos that might be out there from my abuser and the torment of never knowing. "Please tell me they aren't real," I beg softly.

"Facial recognition software has connected ten to various snuff films. Five were attached to solved pedophile cases. Morgan said she would forward the information to the victim's lawyers. They would be entitled to sue anyone housing their photo. Seven of the girls in this folder are underage. I sent those names to sex crimes. If they match any of their open cases, it might kick back some information or put another victim on their radar."

A series of images draw my attention as Karina and Sydney continue to talk. A young girl, maybe ten, her light brown hair in pigtails and wearing a blue one-piece bathing suit, fills the screen. Her smile is wide as she runs through a sprinkler on a front lawn. The image was probably taken from across the street. The images continue to switch, getting closer to the young girl as she plays in her driveway or walks to school. Then they turn dark. She holds her knees to her chest, her arms and legs bare, her face contorted with fear and tears. She grows up on the screen, dolled up and standing in front of a cheap backdrop. Her face ages with her body, but the eyes—the empty blue eyes—remain the same. I pray this girl, now a woman, was rescued and given proper therapy to survive her ordeal.

"That's Tanika Entils. She's one of the solved cases, thankfully. The DA on her case requested more information as they're pursuing restitution. It's not a consolation, but it can help her to start over after . . . all of this."

"Only to be violated again and again when some new freak gets caught with these images." I shake my head in disgust. "That's if they even pay, which we know they probably won't. "

"It's not perfect, but if successful, it allows the victim to get long-term help. That's most important." Sydney continues trying to make me see some of the positives and reduce my desire to castrate these people.

"And he has more folders like this?" Karina says, walking closer to the screen, the intrigue evident on her face. "How did he go undetected for all this time?

"Any number of reasons," Sydney pipes up.

I cut into the conversation, needing to leave as soon as possible. "Keep working and let me know what else comes through." The pressure in my chest increases with each step, my breathing shallow, and I feel a cold sweat forming on my skin. Popping open the top button of my shirt, I try to count to ten with every gasp of oxygen. A tech exits the elevator and looks at me awkwardly. It makes my brain move into overdrive. My hands shake as I pull out my cell phone and dial as fast as my numb fingers allow.

"Hello?" The groggy voice comes back through the line.

"Hey, it's Detective Steele. I need . . ." The words fail me.

"I'll see you in a few minutes." The call ends before I can even put the words together in a coherent sentence.

Stepping inside the elevator, I hear Karina calling after me.

"You okay?" Her eyes scan over my body, taking in the sweat, tremors, and appearance of withdrawal. "Maybe you should sit down and have some water. It's going to be a long night . . . if you're up for it."

I hit the number for the garage level and lean against the cold back wall, putting some distance between us. I feel a bead of sweat roll between my breasts as I'm still unable to stop my breathing from being so weak.

"I'll be back. Need to handle something. Check ballistics with Dr. Brown and see if the bullet gave us anything. I shouldn't be long."

The doors close and lead to the mostly empty garage level. My hands fumble to unlock my driver's side door. The minute I'm safely inside, I lose control. Tears fall, and my hand slams the steering wheel over and over again. A scream bubbles from deep within me.

"Stop it, stop it . . ." The voice sounds foreign and weak. My fists curl and hit the side of my head, and my knees hit the bottom of the steering wheel. "Stop it, please, stop it . . . I don't want to think about it."

It feels like I'm outside my body. I'm sitting in the back seat watching myself as I break down. The numbness overtakes every inch of me. Thankfully, the keys are resting in the cup holder and not in the ignition. There's no driving until my breathing stabilizes. The attack needs to pass. I've never been good with patience.

***

Standing outside the door, my breathing barely under control, I press the doorbell. My hair feels wet and stuck to my face. My entire being aches like I've run a marathon with no training. The door opens, and Dr. Preston stands there in her Wynonna Earp pajamas and Tardis slippers. If I weren't such a mess, I'd ask where she got them.

She says nothing as I'm ushered into her office and helped into the chair I've claimed as my own. The muted darkness from the dimmed lights envelops me with kindness and a bit of serenity. I feel my body rocking, my hands shaking as I try to stop everything running through my veins. My shirt is wet with sweat, my face stained with salty tears, and I have no control over it all.

I hear her come back in and sit on the coffee table between us. She places a cold glass of water in my hand and helps me take a few sips before my fingers release it. She places it down before breathing loudly. Her breaths in are deep, and she exhales slowly through her mouth. I know what she's doing and why, and I try to follow her rhythm. I need to slow my breathing down before I end up in the hospital next to my friends.

Deep breath. Hold. Purse lips and release while counting to ten. Repeat. I don't know how long I follow that mantra in my head, but it helps. Every breath pushes the anxiety back in a corner. The exhales help my heart slow and my mind focus on one thing. It's simple, and I've made Chase do it many times before, but it calms me to a functioning level.

"I'm sorry. I didn't know who else to call."

"Where's Frankie?" she asks softly.

"At the hospital with Chase. He, ahh . . . he wanted to stay with his aunt, so they're gonna stay the night."

"Have you called her at all?"

"No." My eyes focus on the floor. "I don't want . . ." I wish I knew what words to say. "I don't want her to know."

"You're okay telling me?"

A humorless laugh rumbles from my chest as tears continue to fall on their own accord. "I'm a detective. I'm an adult. This . . . none of this should bother me anymore."

"What does?"

"The last case. Everything got triggered from there, and I want it to go away. Be locked back up and not have to think about it anymore."

"Jasmine, listen to me carefully. We lock things away so we don't have to face them. It's a safety mechanism and is perfectly normal. You said you were triggered? What happened?"

"I umm . . . went to the bar where I saw him last." The name sticks in my throat like peanut butter. "Mr. Lemont."

"Who was he?"

"A friend's father." I reach for the water again, my throat dry and scratchy. Jenette keeps her hands below mine as they still have a slight shake to them. After I take in half the glass in a few gulps, she pulls it back and sets it down on the table. "Everyone thought he was the best dad in the neighborhood. He had this Mustang he always worked on. He'd lie on the ground and teach all the boys about it. God, they all loved him. Fucking stupid."

"Why was it stupid?"

"They listened to everything he said, thrived on his actions . . ." I rub my nose against my sleeve, giving myself a break.

"What did he do?" Jenette softly pries.

"Anything he wanted." I force my body to stand and put some distance between the doctor and myself. Looking out at the darkened park, I wonder how many people will be hurt without proper lighting. "This new case . . . there were images of this little girl. Her eyes . . . they were so alive when she was little. Vibrant and innocent, you know? I watched image after image as she got older and those same eyes became lifeless. Someone took her innocence away and left her a shell of herself."

"Those are difficult things to see."

"Nah, doc, I can handle seeing things like that because it means we're investigating it. I can handle dead bodies on the floor because it means we're trying to catch the piece of shit that did it."

"Then why did this little girl bother you?"

"She grew up like that, being abused and made up for some adult's sick pleasure."

"You just said that seeing those images were simply part of the case."

"Don't think I'm a sick fuck or immoral. Seeing that shit day in and out would screw me up beyond belief. I don't know how Special Victims does it, the constant . . . I couldn't do it."

"There is no judgment in this room, but aren't you doing that to yourself? What is it about that little girl that bothered you so much, detective?"

The question fills the room with silence. To answer it means to open Pandora's Box to a human being I barely know. It also means allowing that same trunk to be broken open with no ability to close it. I feel my soul screaming to be cleansed but my head begging me not to in the same breath. The concerns and negative effects rise like hives on my skin. The doctor could tell my captain that I'm not fit for active duty. I could lose my badge, something that defines the very fiber of my being.

"I was her." The words taste like acid on my tongue. The woman says nothing. I assume she's waiting for me to finish my thoughts, but they're so tangential I couldn't speak if I wanted to. I've admitted something to this person that has never come out of my mouth. Frankie knew bits and pieces, but I've never had to say it. She just pulled me into her arms and wiped the tears away. "I am her." The words come out a little bit louder this time.

I wrap my hand around the small necklace Frankie gave me on our seventh anniversary—the small stones in a heart, something more feminine than I would normally wear. My other hand presses on the glass for stability. I breathe in deeply, counting to ten as I exhale. I focus on my breathing as I try to gather my thoughts. "My favorite bathing suit growing up was this blue one-piece with the Coca-Cola logo on it. The logo was red with some glitter or something. Georgie and I were inseparable growing up, and we always loved to try and stand on the pool floats. We always fell, but we were kids, ya know? You do stupid shit to stay entertained."

I hear the doc behind me move to the couch. I look over my shoulder to verify that's all she's doing. My vulnerability is getting the better of my trust at the moment.

"Her dad, Mr. Lemont, he would pick us up and throw us in the water. He was strong enough that it felt like we were flying."

"Sounds like you had fun," Jenette adds.

"It was. Until it wasn't. That's always the case, though, right? One day that same man you trust corners you on a ladder to the loft of the garage. He pushes you against the steps and kisses you while you're holding the unicorn float. One minute you're this happy kid, and the next you're confused about what's happening."

"You were a child . . ."

"I should have known better. I could have gone home and told my parents. I should have—"

"What do you tell victims of sexual assault?"

"I'm supposed to be stronger, better, the protector . . . not some frail adult hiding in her memories, doc. I shouldn't remember or focus on what his hands felt like on me or inside me. I should be able to shut that shit down. Instead, I can smell his fucking cigars again, and now it's making me crazy. I should have fucking known better."

I let my necklace fall loosely around my neck; both my hands are holding me up against the cold glass.

"Detective, what happened to you has made you stronger as you put it. But if you don't process it, then you won't be able to move beyond it. You deserve to heal and move on."

"I don't know what I deserve." I push off the glass and begin to pace around the office. "Frankie would wake me up from these shitty nightmares when we first started dating and hold me. She never asked any questions. She deserves someone stronger, or at least an explanation. I mean—fuck, she married me already." I stop and rest my hands on the back of the chair. "Did you know I still can't sleep without some light in the room? Yeah, Frankie needs everything to be pitch-black, but if I'm in the dark, I cringe. Like I fall back into this panic anxiety bullshit of being hurt. So, there's my nightlight on the fucking end table like I'm nine years old again!" My voice cuts off as I feel myself losing what little control I had over this session.

Jenette sits on the couch, her legs crossed as she leans back into it. No notebook in sight. I look around the room, trying to find where the tape recorder might be hiding.

"There's nothing, detective. I told you this is a safe space."

My cell phone vibrates, and it takes me a few seconds to register the movement on my belt.

"Hello?" I answer, my voice still a bit shaky.

"Jasmine, you need to be here. Now," Frankie says coldly over the line before disconnecting it. I shove my phone back into the holster, chug the water, and head to the front door.

"Detective, are you okay to drive?" I hear Jenette walking behind me, her footsteps quick as she tries to catch up. "Detective . . ."

"I have to be; they need me at the hospital. I'll be back for our scheduled session. I give you my word." I swing the front door open, skip the elevator, and take the stairs three at a time.

***

At the hospital, the elevator door opens to chaos. Police officers remain along the walls, out of the way. Alarms blare from the speakers, waking up all the other patients on the floor. Stepping out, I'm almost run over by a nurse rushing down the hallway. That's when Hadley's screams hit my ears. Her words are indiscernible from the other voices in the vicinity.

My legs move of their own accord, my long strides taking me around the corner and down the hallway. The captain jumps in front of me to stop my motion. He tries to talk to me, but my vision is focused on the lump of three people I love on the floor. Frankie and Chase hold Hadley from behind as she continues to fight them. An officer stoically holds the IV bag above her, but even he is feeling the emotions from her wails.

I walk past them all and into the room. Logan lies motionless on the bed. His left arm hangs off the side as one doctor compresses his chest while a nurse pushes air into his lungs.

"Clear."

The command rings out before everyone moves away from Logan's prone form. The sound of the discharge of electricity pops in my ears. His body rises from the bed, his hands forming fists into the sheets. Once his back hits the sheets, the doctor continues compressions with the nurse squeezing a bag rhythmically.

"Charging," the other doctor says.

Zeile slides into the room and stands next to me, hands clasped in front of him, waiting.

"How long?"

"Five or ten minutes. They've already shocked him twice."

"Clear." Once again people move away from Logan's body as the paddles press against his chest. The pop of electricity hits, and he seems impossibly higher off the bed. It takes a few seconds longer before his back hits the mattress again. The other two continue their lifesaving tactics.

One doctor places the paddles back in the defibrillator. He watches the other two continue their movements before glancing over to the monitors.

"Stop compressions," he says, and everyone stops.

The heartbeat is the only sound in the room as even Hadley's cries have subsided. *Lub-dub, lub-dub, lub-dub . . . lub-dub . . . lub-dub . . . lub . . . dub . . . lub . . . flatline.*

Hadley emits a sound I've never heard before as the doctors discuss the time of death. They lift the white sheet and pull it over his head. The doctors turn all the machines off, silencing the flatline. I turn and see all the officers in the hallway take their hats off one by one.

Kneeling, I pull Hadley to me in a tight hug. Her arms wrap around me tightly as her tears soak my shirt. I vaguely hear the captain talking to the staff behind us. I feel Chase hug her from the right while Frankie swarms us from the left.

"Steele? Medical personnel need to check her over," Zeile whispers to me over the scene. I nod in response, knowing they will want to check to see if she's done any damage to herself or ripped her stitches. I'll help her back to a room in a minute, but right now we're not going anywhere.

Chapter Thirteen

It's been four days since Logan's death, and the media is still running wild with theories. Hadley plans to go back to work following the service. Her recently hired bodyguards shadow her every move. All of her scenes were moved indoors, and she no longer indulges in any fan interactions. The new studio hires ensure she's safe, but primarily make sure that no one talks to her. From what I understand, every interview must be cleared by the producers before she agrees. No one wants her talking about this case.

The rest of us keep pushing forward, trying to connect Barrett to Logan's murder and Hadley's shooting.

The bullet had residue on it that matched the same polymer from his job. The schematics were found in his encrypted folders. No witnesses. No smoking gun. Victor did the autopsy to ensure nothing was missed. The cause of death was confirmed to be a lack of oxygen to the brain due to an allergic reaction. He told us all that Logan was most likely brain dead before the machines were ever turned on. It removed a little bit of guilt from Will and me but never removed the emptiness. Beyond that, Logan was healthy and showed no signs of foul play. Of all the solved crimes in the file cabinets, this was the most perfect and most frustrating.

"What the fuck is this shit?" I slam the newspaper on Morgan's desk. The image of Barrett, Cunning, Boner/Hucek, and Catz in handcuffs covers the front page. The headline "Pornography Ring Broken" covers the top in bold letters.

"It's the *New York Post*. Anyone with a brain cell reads the *New York Times* in this city," she says, pushing the paper away from her court documents. "You might want to reconsider your tone and how you enter a room, detective. It's unbecoming of a person in your position."

"Position? This piece of shit murdered a member of the NYPD and attempted to kill Hadley. You sit here in your fancy office in your pretentious pin-striped suit like you own the place, but you can't do your damn job!" My voice bellows down the hallway, alerting others to the argument inside.

Morgan moves around her desk, her heels click clacking across the floor, and slams her door shut. Within seconds, she's in my face, her chest puffed in anger.

"Listen here, detective, before you go off the deep end and say more than you already have. I am not a woman who toys with people, nor am I someone who runs off at the mouth. I get my hands dirty when needed, and I get a conviction where and when I can."

"You should be prosecuting him for murder, attempted murder, and stalking. Your 'getting a conviction where you can' is a crock of shit. You're scared to take this to the jury."

"With what evidence? You want me to present, give me something! You gave me nothing but—"

"We gave you everything we had!" My voice cuts her off.

"Which was nothing!" she replies.

"You had the guts to destroy Karina's career, but you don't dare do this? You're in the wrong fucking job then." The words come out before I can stop my anger. The minute they're in the ether, I wish I could take them back.

Morgan's face is fixed, but her eyes show how deeply those words cut her. She raises her hands in the air and takes a few steps back, shaking her head. I try to move forward, but she points a finger at me and motions to the chair. Without saying another word, I sit down, and my right leg starts bouncing, the energy flowing through my body pulsing out with each twitch of movement.

Morgan sits down at her desk and pushes in her chair. She pulls on the bottom drawer and grabs a small bottle of whiskey and two glasses. She pours a little bit inside each before closing the bottle back up. The two of us sit, staring at the glasses, waiting for the other to speak.

Morgan breaks the silence, her right index finger playing with the rim of the glass. "The Seattle Slayer was the most difficult case I've ever taken on. We had nothing, and Agent Marlow . . . Karina was working so hard. She had these binders full of evidence. It was her meticulous work that made my job easy in the end."

"How did you know it was Simon?"

"He slipped up. It was by the Space Needle; he was in the background of a tourist's pictures on social media. Tech was searching facial recognition and several posts came up. I didn't see it at first; neither did Karina. Our bosses made me sort through all her shit line by line."

"They took her out of action."

"Me as well, indirectly." She nudges the glass and swirls the fluid around. "They sent me a text message later asking me to keep Karina busy. Apparently, they served a search warrant and found his hidden keepsakes. Her boys were terrified, and I was the reason she wasn't there. The powers that be put us in each other's way, and now we're both here."

"You're in New York. I don't see that as an issue."

"I wanted to be in Washington, DC, making a difference. This job is nothing to sniff at, but once again, Karina and I are at odds."

"Sit down and talk it out with her. Explain everything and maybe find some common ground. You're going to be working with all of us for the foreseeable future, so things like Simon can't come between us and this bust. And it can't happen without communication."

"You do realize I do not, nor will I ever, answer to you or the team," she says flatly.

"No, but as a human being, and a team member, you need us as much as we need you. You want us to listen to you, we only ask for the same."

Morgan releases the glass and leans back in the chair. She opens her drawer and pulls out a file. "You never saw this, you understand?"

I nod and reach for the folder, open it, and see papers containing a ton of legalese. "What am I looking at?"

"I had no choice but to bring Thomas Catz in. We seized his computer and found an interesting collection of videos of underage girls. Apparently, this perfect young man shot uniformed schoolgirl porn after school. He even stars in some of them. He posted these files to that forum and exchanged it for cash. He's agreed to roll on everyone he knows in that forum if we reduce the sentences. He's looking at twenty to forty years, and yes, that's reduced. I wanted to charge him ten years per file, but he'd be out in the next millennia."

"We interviewed him."

"And asked him about what you were investigating: Hadley and Logan. The forum was a bonus, but not for your case. It happens."

"What about Cunning and the rest?"

"Demanding trial, but the evidence is damning. That and Catz's testimony. He's done for."

"None of this explains—"

"I talked to my superiors with what we had. You gave me an amazing amount of circumstantial evidence that may or may not have gotten a conviction, let alone an indictment." Morgan reaches forward and takes the file from my hands. She searches through all the pages before she pulls one out and hands it to me. There is a list of charges that take up half the page. Some I recognize, but others are new.

"What's this?"

"A laundry list of federal as well as state-level crimes that will put Barrett away for life. With all the factual evidence, the testimony of others, and the tech department, he won't get out. I can confidently say this is the best way to handle it. That doesn't mean we won't look into or keep working on Logan and Hadley's case. It simply means we have to hold off for a bit."

"The tax evasion angle."

"If you're referring to Al Capone, yes. I know you're very close to this case, but take a step back and look at the bigger picture."

"What if Barrett makes a deal. Immunity for more names from that forum or something juicer?"

"It's always a possibility. I've spoken to my old colleagues, and it is something they are looking into. They've also said he will serve time in a federal prison no matter what. Unless he's offering up a terrorism plot or something of that level, they won't plead down to probation or less."

"You can't guarantee that."

"No, I can't. But I also know they don't appreciate individuals who are under investigation for murdering one of their own."

I get up, all the steam from my earlier entrance is gone. Morgan stands as well, waiting to see what I'm going to do next. I place the paper back on her side of the desk, slam the whiskey in one gulp, and enjoy the burn all the way down. She slides hers in front of me.

"You're off duty and heading into an emotional day. Take it."

Without a second thought, I take the shot and relish the continued burning. The small amount of liquor won't help the situation or dull my senses, but it gives me a false sense of calm. "You're on the clock, I get it."

"No. I don't drink. Never have," she says, pushing both glasses to the side of her desk. "It's my father's drink," she says before sitting back down, folding up the case file, and looking back to her laptop.

"There's a story there."

"There always is, detective. This one is for another day. Try not to break my door on the way out?" She smirks, sliding her glasses down her nose and giving me a stern look. "And Steele?"

I stop in the doorway, my back to her. "Please find something to change my mind." I turn quickly and see Morgan's focus is back to the papers in front of her. She's given us more time. Maybe she isn't as bad as she seems.

***

My scratchy dress blues make every inch of my skin crawl. Reporters hover outside, flash photography blinding everyone walking in or out. Thankfully, the funeral home has allowed Hadley to use the employee entrance.

"Detective Steele, any comment?"

"How's Hadley handling it?"

"Will she continue shooting?"

The questions fire at me from the moment I step out of the car. The metal barricades put up by the nearby precinct prevent them from getting too close. The line of blue blocks many of their photos as well. All of the plainclothes officers face those entering the building, their backs to the masses. It's a calming effect in the craziness surrounding the wake. The press leaked the details too close to the date to switch everything. The captain handled as much as possible as Frankie, Victor, and I took care of our friend.

The inside of the building is much of the same. The low murmurs of conversation fill every nook and cranny of the place. The majority of people are dressed in suits, uniforms, and other formal attire. As I walk through the crowd, people move out of my way quickly. They know where I'm headed, albeit I'm late as usual.

The room on the left is overflowing with people. The faux walls are pushed back to allow the entire side to be used. Every chair is occupied except the front row. The nicer, cushioned ones are for family, as if this alleviates any of their grief. All it does is remind you it's your family in that box.

Frankie stands in the front in a black dress and heels, her long. blonde curls cascading over her shoulders. She finds me in the crowd and gives me a small smile. Hugging the wall, I manage to make it to her in a few steps. Three people I've never met before sit to the right of Hadley. They talk to one another, sometimes smiling and laughing lightly.

Hadley seems undisturbed by the actions around her. The studio probably chose her black designer suit. Her eyes are red, her face puffy as she stares at the box in front of her. She sits with perfect posture, legs crossed and completely shut down.

"How long has she been like this?"

"Varying degrees since the hospital," Frankie whispers in my ear. "She sat down the moment we got here and hasn't moved. People have tried to talk to her, but it's like she doesn't see them."

"It's because all she sees is him."

The front wall is lined with easels of flowers, boards filled with pinned images, and a small table with a simple cherrywood box. His gaming headset rests on top of the box with an Xbox controller to the right. On the left is an image of Logan and Hadley in a candid moment, the two smiling to the point of laughter, eyes squeezed shut in a rare moment of peace.

Logan's will had requested he be cremated—no funeral, and no wake. He wanted a small dinner for those he cared about and for all of us to move on. Considering the case and the press coverage, that was one part of his wish no one could abide by. The entire department wanted to grieve, and they decided to hold a full ceremony. The captain arranged the viewing, much to Hadley's discontent.

"Where's Chase?"

"In the other room with Mia and the girls. We didn't think it would be smart for them to be on this side, but they wanted to be here."

"Optics shouldn't overshadow this."

"You're not the one causing the storm of paparazzi outside."

Understanding washes over me, and I kiss Frankie on the cheek before sitting on Hadley's left. The chair is so familiar to me. as if my body has molded to the stiffness of the back. The images of my grandparents, parents, brother, sister-in-law, and Captain Tyler Udall flash before my eyes, knowing we're born with such fanfare and, in most cases, go out of this world with little to none.

I place my hand on the armrest of Hadley's chair directly next to hers. In seconds, I feel her hand cover mine, our fingers lacing together as they have so many times throughout our friendship. When my mother died, she sat to my left and made the same motion. The simplicity of it, knowing someone is there who understood what I needed—no platitudes, just companionship.

The funeral director walks to a podium in the front right of the room. The small structure, hidden among the flowers, cards, and photos, emits a short squeal as the microphone turns on. I feel Hadley's hand tighten in mine as her eyes shut and she takes a deep breath. The man talks to the crowd, but my focus stays on my friend and her inability to cope or grieve properly.

One by one, people walk up to the podium and share stories. The people on the other side of Hadley turn out to be Rebecca, Charlie, and Akuni, Logan's longtime friends and gaming buddies. They flew in from all across the country to be here, and if not for the woman next to me, I would be listening to them.

After each person speaks, they kneel in front of Hadley. They all take her right hand, say something, kiss her on the forehead, and move on. None of them notice her eyes are empty or unfocused. None of them realize or care that she isn't responding to anyone verbally. Her family—Frankie, Victor, and me—accept the silence and remain firm in our places around her. We are blocking the overwhelming stimuli from hitting her hard.

There's a long procession of speakers, including Zeile and Will, who broke down a few times before he handed Hadley his Purple Heart medal in honor of Logan. That very medal presses into my free hand with something else: pieces of paper folded so small to fit in my palm. I wonder if she's been holding onto these for the entire session. Her head turns, and the tears slowly streaking down as everything slowly sinks in.

No words need to be spoken as I rise to my feet and drag myself over to the podium. For some reason, people must think I'm stronger than I actually am. I did a eulogy at my grandmother's funeral, my brother's, and most recently, Captain Udall's. All of them were powerful and emotionally draining, yet this one feels the most important. I've been able to hide what I've felt in those words on the paper. Like a teacher giving a lesson, one can bury their tears behind each syllable as they breathe. Standing there, unfolding the pages, I doubt I will be able to do that this time. Looking over at Hadley, I see Frankie holds her hand in my place, but her eyes are solely on me. I decide to start reading right away to prevent my grief from taking hold of her words.

"Hadley has asked that I read this for her: First, let me thank you all for being here to celebrate Logan today. Secondly, I apologize for having Jasmine speak for me. Although she speaks well, knowing some of you work with her, I'm sure you want to scream for her to shut up now and again." The crowd laughs lightly. "Finally, although everyone is here for the man of the hour, he would have hated it. In fact, this is the one thing he never felt was necessary. This pomp and circumstance of a life gone well before its time only to be forgotten in the coming years. He would have preferred we all logged into a game and blew everything up in his name." The crowd chuckles again.

"But that's only the tip of the iceberg when it comes to the man I knew. Once a fanboy who just wanted to watch all my movies with me, always skipping the nudity or sex scenes because he was more embarrassed than I was, he never viewed me for my physique, or my name, my bank account, or, later on, my fame. He looked at me and saw the girl who wanted to be seen and loved."

I read the next line and my eyes widen in shock. Hadley sits there, tears rolling down consistently now, and raises her eyebrows at me. "To explain who Logan was, I have to refer to the night he proposed to me. We were in Colorado for one of my press engagements. Even though he was a tech and gamer guy, he loved to share the simpler things with me. After a morning of interviews and without any coffee, I was standing in fleece-lined pants, a ski jacket, sunglasses, and snowshoes. We followed this path through the trees, enjoying everything from the animals to seeing where the state quarter's image came from. Even in the beauty of Mother Nature, Logan was always a child at heart. There, in the middle of a clearing, ice as far as the eye can see, he built a little snowman."

My voice hitches and I force it back down. I feel like I'm intruding on a private moment that was meant for the two of them.

"He placed his hat on its head and wrapped his scarf around its neck. He had a whole speech written out but was shaking so much he couldn't read it. So, he improvised, telling me that the snowman was braver than he was. It would stand tall and fight against the sun even when it knew the inevitable melting would happen. He said that little guy in the middle of the glacier had more courage than he did because he had to sum up how he felt about me in one line. No matter what he could design, code, or encrypt, nothing would be enough to explain how much I was it for him.

"He fell to his knees in front of me and held out a small diamond ring. He asked me to be his co-op player in the game of life. If not for my nephew, I would have no idea what he meant to this day. I just knew I wanted to marry him, be with him, and fight against the inevitability of the 'game over' screen. You're probably a bit lost, so let me explain. He always put life in the frame of a game. Loads of adventures until a horde of zombies surround you and you run out of bullets. Ergo, the inevitable 'game over' screen."

The crowd chuckles softly as I clear my throat. Will hands me a small cup of water, and I take a sip to fight the dryness but also the emotion rattling through my being.

"Yet, here I sit without my fiancé, who never became my husband. I want to say we fought, but someone took our future away. For that, I will always feel cheated. But being with Logan, for however short a time it was, shall remain one of the greatest times of my life. I pray there is an afterlife, and he's simply making sure the Wi-Fi is working for when I get there."

People chuckle while others blow their noses. I try to make out the final words, as the page is smeared with dried tears. "I pray everyone here knows how much Logan truly loved everyone he came across. His kind, jovial spirit lives in all of us. For me, his love has made me a stronger person. His support made me follow my outlandish dreams to fruition. I will spend the rest of my life remembering the little things, the calm moments, and his soft snores as I continue to fight against the inevitable for him."

***

Karina and I have been working diligently in the basement since the wake. Will made sure Hadley took something to rest through the night. The entire chosen family is staying at my house. Maybe for safety, but primarily for comfort.

"I've got something!" Dr. Brown rushes into our office holding a piece of paper above her head. "There were several fibers on the bullet. I cross-referenced it with Hadley's clothing and excluded those. If we can find that sweatshirt, I can match it."

"I wish we could, Lil. Morgan gave us a short window before she sits down with Barrett's lawyers."

"Not to mention the federal government will be scooping him up in the early morning hours," Karina adds. "We need something in the evidence we already have."

"Is he out on bail?" I ask.

"Yes, rather quickly after his hearing. Why?" Lillian answers.

"I just need five minutes," I growl.

"No. If we do this, we do it the right way."

Sydney walks into the room and places her laptop in the center of my desk. Her fingers fly over the keys as I try to retrieve some of the papers underneath it. She swats my hand away.

"He listed his Mike Piazza World Series autographed baseball on Craigslist. Cash only," she answers. "He's trying to run."

"He's got enough cash; he could do that anyway," Lillian adds.

"Not if Morgan seized his passport and froze his accounts after he posted bond. We're stupid; he's a classic flight risk, avoids confrontation. He needs cash to get out of the area," I answer quickly. "How much is he asking for?"

"Ten thousand." Sydney answers.

"Tell him nine and he's got a deal." I begin to pace the length of the room.

"You don't have that kind of money," Karina interjects before stepping in my path. "Nor can we justify it or get it so soon."

"No, but we can get a confession," I answer. "But it means someone he doesn't recognize has to go into the lion's den." I turn my attention to Lillian, and she shifts from foot to foot nervously.

"We are not putting her into the field with no training, Steele." Karina shuts down my thought process immediately. "What if he has no intention of selling that damn thing? What if he has another printed weapon and doesn't miss this time? This might be a setup for suicide by cop before he has to go to prison. It's not a risk I'd be willing to take."

"He hasn't been back to work since we interviewed his associate. In fact, his best buddy CEO put him on paid leave. He has no access to those machines or materials," I counter.

"I'll do it," Lillian whispers so low that my ears don't fully register what she's saying.

"That's a calculated risk. Again, we've just lost a member of this team, and you want to put another one in harm's way before Logan's body is even in an urn?" Karina's face is etched with worry as her hands move about in grand gestures.

"It's my choice!" Lillian raises her voice, stopping our argument in its tracks. "I'll do it, but I need to know you'll all be nearby."

"Lillian, he could attack you . . ."

"I grew up with three brothers. If he lays a hand on me, I know how to get away. It'll be long enough for you to put him in the ground."

Karina stares at Lillian, trying to assuage her fears or convince the doctor to step down. Neither one budges in their determination. Karina walks to her desk, opens the top drawer, and pulls out a small pinky-finger-length blade.

"You're smart. Hit him where it would do the most damage."

Lillian takes the blade and nods vigorously. The two women are coming to an understanding over the worst situation possible. I can see Lillian swallow harshly, and I rub her back gently. She shrugs me off as we wait.

"Eleven p.m., Riverside Park's Hippo Playground," Sydney says, cutting through the tension.

"That gives us two hours to form our plan, get ready, and get there."

"Reinforcements?" Sydney asks.

"The rest of the team is at my house protecting everyone," I answer.

"Captain Zeile was called into FBI Headquarters downtown. I doubt he'd make it, and we're on a skeleton shift due to the earlier services."

"You're saying it's just us then?" Sydney asks.

"No," I answer. "We'll call the local precinct in the area and tell them to ensure the park is sealed. We can't have anyone wandering around that late at night. It's a kid's section; theoretically it should be empty."

Sydney pulls up the map on Google and some corresponding images: the small hippo statues on black pavement along with a few benches and a jungle gym. Scanning over the image, I point to a bench near a small set of bushes in the middle of the park.

"Sydney can hide in there. Those three bushes are packed tightly together. You stay close to the ground and keep your eyes on him. He does anything, you shoot," I say, waving my finger around the cluster of cover.

"Right, put the Black girl in the dirt. I'll blend in," Sydney says. I raise my hand to counter, but she cuts me off. "It's just one of the stupid things they'd say on the beat. Blending in is my best asset." She shrugs.

"You're small enough to fit there, and you're a good shot. That's why I want you there. I know you won't hesitate."

Sydney nods and falls into my chair. "Lillian should be wired."

"Of course. Simple sale in a park. Hook me up. Why should I worry about that?" Lillian asks.

"Because he's in all the papers and listed it on fucking Craigslist. He's not thinking straight. I'm sure everyone has already seen this posting," Karina answered.

"He probably isn't in his right frame of mind. We all know what other inmates do to convicted pedophiles. It won't end well for the man who runs from conflict," I add.

"Not anymore," Sydney answers, drawing our attention to her. The website page shows a "could not find" message. "He pulled it once we accepted. It was only up for an hour tops."

"Still enough to cause concern," Karina continues. "Okay. Steele, you hide in the bushes by the entrance. If he makes a run for it, you take him out."

"And you?" I ask.

"I'll be opposite the bench, hiding in the bushes by the hippo statues."

"So, how do I trap him?" Lillian asks honestly. "I mean, not everyone has nine thousand dollars lying around their houses. I need to have a story about that if he asks."

"You've been stocking money away out of every paycheck since 2008 happened. Cash is king, and this would be a huge gift for your father's birthday. It was worth dipping into the reserves to get it," I answer.

"I don't know if I should be impressed or worried by how quickly you can lie," Lillian says.

"You need to ask him questions about the baseball. Why would you be doing this shady deal at night in the park alone? You're a woman with a ton of cash on her person. You will be armed and ready for him. He has to prove he's not a threat and that the ball is authentic. We've all seen the papers; you can play off that. He 'looks' like that criminal who screws little girls. He might be talkative and spill, who knows," Karina continues.

"It's ten fifteen," Sydney cuts in, and just like that, we're out of time.

Chapter Fourteen

The park is cold and empty this late in the evening. The Twenty-Second Precinct is running a few more passes in this area for coverage in case we need them—nothing overly dramatic to cause Barrett to run away, just enough to look normal. At least we hope. Frankie's been calling, but as we all get ready, earpieces firmly in place, we all shut down our phones. We can't risk the noise or light going off and triggering him.

Lillian walks around the hippos, bouncing around like a little kid in a candy store with a small reusable bag on her shoulder. She's trying to look excited about this evening's "drug deal," but we all know it's nervous energy. The rustling of leaves fills my ears as the wind blows through the trees. I'm a good distance away, but I can see everything from my hiding spot. If it goes south, I'll be on him before he knows what to do.

A man in a black hoodie walks into the park. It has to be Barrett. His shoulders are hunched forward, his shoes are scraping the pavement as he walks, and his hands are in the kangaroo pocket of his sweatshirt. I doubt this is the intelligent and savvy man from earlier in the day. This is a man afraid of the law and the ramifications of his actions.

Lillian watches him enter the park and sit on the park bench she was supposed to be on. She leans against a statue and watches him.

"You here about the ball?" he grunts.

"You here about the money?" She laughs. "I wouldn't be hanging out in a kid's park this time of night for my health."

Barrett stands quickly and lurches in her direction. Lillian pulls out Karina's knife quickly and holds her ground. He slowly sits back down.

"No reason to get testy."

"Forgive me, but I'm a woman of color in the middle of a park in the dead of night. I think my weaponry is acceptable given those circumstances."

"Do you want it or not?"

"Of course, I do. My father is a huge fan, but I'm worried about its authenticity. I replied rather hastily out of excitement." She waves the small blade around for effect. "Bit spontaneous of me or stupid. Not sure at the moment."

"My ex got me the game-used ball from game four of the 2000 World Series. Mike Piazza was signing his books at the old Barnes & Noble on Fifth Avenue. Waited outside in the cold for hours just to get a bracelet with a time to come back. I was part of the first group of people. I had to buy his book too. Paid another hundred bucks under the table to have the ball signed. I remember he was surprised I had one." Barrett shrugs his shoulders at the memory. "That enough for you?"

"I guess. I mean I'm here already, so a simple got it outside of Shea Stadium would have worked fine for me." Lillian rests the small bag on the floor by the hippo. "It's all in there." She motions to it.

But Barrett doesn't move. He looks around but at what I'm not sure. His right hand pulls the baseball in its square plastic case out of the kangaroo pocket. He places it on the bench next to him. Next, he pulls out a certificate of authenticity in a plastic frame.

"You come alone?" he asks, his tone lowering somewhat.

"I don't know if I feel comfortable answering that question. I reiterate the woman of color alone in a park detail," Lillian answers, but I can tell by her movements she's becoming more nervous with every passing second.

Barrett lowers his hoodie and stares at Lillian. From this distance, I can see his left eye is a mess. I assume he picked up something in the holding cells. His demeanor changes, his shoulder appears to tighten, and my gut tells me the situation is changing.

"I just want my money," he states, his voice hard.

"Umm . . . do you know . . ." Lillian stares at him, taking in every aspect of our perp before continuing her thoughts. "You were on the cover of *Post* today." Her voice tapers off as if in disbelief. She's playing it perfectly, but will he rise to the bait?

Barrett looks around again before standing to his full height. He bends his neck to the left, allowing it to pop loudly. "I think you're mistaken." He takes one step toward Lillian. "But if I were him, you should know that I'm not one to mess with. Let's finish this transaction and go . . ." He allows the sentence to hang in the air unfinished.

"You shot Hadley Moreno," Lillian blurts out, and my stomach drops. That was not part of the script. I hear Karina in my ear telling us all to stay put. I assume she is waiting to see how it plays out.

"Now where'd you get that idea?"

"It was online. Twitter said you were . . . that you . . ." She slips as her phrases become more disjointed. "But the news said the person who shot Ms. Moreno also killed her boyfriend . . ." Lillian lets the words hang in the air. She holds the knife out and grabs the bag at her feet. She backs away to another hippo. "I think I'll just go. Forget the ball." She maneuvers around the park toward Karina and the brush.

"I need that money!" he says desperately. The aggression in his voice grows louder as his arms wave around wildly. "Leave the bag, lady. I need . . . just do it."

Lillian ignores him and holds firm a good distance from him. I watch as his shoulders rise and fall with several deep breaths. His hood slides casually back on his head. Karina's voice comes through the earpiece: "Get ready." I see Sydney's shoes move slightly, probably to get a better angle.

"You're making me do this." His voice is low, calm, and cold. "Just like her. Tossing out words for the world to hear but none of it means anything. It breaks you when the woman you love is nothing but a trashy whore with a government lackey. I didn't want to be so out in the open with Hadley. I preferred the slow, painful revenge on her boy toy." He rolls his neck and shoulders. It's pure madness flowing out of him as he prepares to attack. "But she'll always know, yes . . . yes, she will. You can't meet at conventions, hug someone and be kind, and write hearts on photos. It's not right." He stops moving entirely. "Hadley will never forget me now. I'll be in her nightmares. But you . . ." He takes one step forward. "I am your nightmare."

He lunges for Lillian, but she slams the small blade into his leg as she falls over the statue to the ground. Barrett grabs the bag and runs toward me. Karina jumps out of the bushes and checks on Lillian. Sydney rolls back out of hers and radios me. I see him moving toward me with considerable speed. I could kill him with one shot. I could remove the nightmare. I step out of my hiding spot, gun drawn, eyes locked on Barrett as he stops two strides in front of me.

In a blink of an eye, I could do for Hadley what Will did for me. I could wash away the fear that would remain should he live. I could ensure that he'd never be able to stalk my friend or my family ever again. With one little bullet, the world would make more sense.

But would it?

Karina hangs back with Sydney and Lillian, watching me. Barrett, bleeding down his pants, stands waiting for me to do something. He stays there like a deer in front of a hunter, unmoving. I take two steps forward, gun still raised, and line up my sights on the center of his forehead. He's eight feet away. It's a sure thing from this close.

"Steele." Karina's voice echoes around me. "Don't give him the luxury of death."

I stare at Barrett one last time. "Get on your knees, hands on your head. Now!" He slumps onto his knees and raises his hands and places them on his head. I take two quick steps forward and unleash a kick Mia Hamm would be proud of, connecting with his groin. He falls hard to his face into the grass. He looks up at me with a smug smile on his face before I pistol-whip him unconscious. Karina shakes her head as she cuffs him and calls the local cops on the watch. I didn't want his death on my conscience. Let the inmates have the sexual predator.

"You shouldn't have done that," Karina tells me. "I'm going to have to write it in the report."

"I fully expect you to," I answer. "You okay?" I ask Lillian.

"Shaken, but still above ground," she answers as Sydney holds her upright.

"You're going to be disciplined, Jasmine. You ready for that?"

I shrug my shoulders and throw it up to the universe. I'm already in therapy, and maybe that anger management class would do me some good. At this point in my life, I, too, want to be above ground with my family. I don't think that's too much to ask.

***

Chase runs through the park with his friends from school. Will continues to grill while parents keep one eye on their kids. Balloons wishing Chase a happy birthday rise from the benches and the pile of gifts. Mia and the girls sit at one and organize all the food so the ravenous children can easily grab some and sit down. Everything is in order.

Hadley plays Frisbee with Chase and his friends. It's been a little over a year since Logan left us, and it's only now that her smile peeks into everyday life. One week after the service, she insisted on getting back to work. The studio was happy to get back on track, but the rest of us worried about her ability to heal and move on. From what I understand, this superhero film is some of her best work. Maybe it was due to her raw emotions in the scenes that required it.

The sun still shines through the trees of the park on this warmer-than-average April day, but the uncertainty of the future does as well. As promised, Karina did write an honest and complete report. I took anger management classes for four months. The report is a permanent mark in my personal file. I've continued with therapy, and it seems to be helping. I don't want to admit it to Frankie, but I started sleeping through the night about two months ago. I'm sure she noticed since my tablet's bright light doesn't keep her awake at odd hours.

I think the biggest change has been the connection between Hadley and Chase. Against my better judgment, we invested in a bunk bed for his room. Aunt Hadley was more than thrilled to move in with the little squirt. With Logan's games, controllers, and whatever else, the two of them bonded more than before. I've also been fired from my zombie playing days. He's got a new, *much better than you, Mom*, co-op player.

"You think she's going to be okay?" Frankie asks, sitting on the bench next to me. I automatically wrap my around her and pull her into my chest.

"No, but he has a cell phone now. They'll keep in touch as much as possible. Lord knows she'll send him pictures from the set or wherever she is." I kiss the top of her head before turning back to the kids.

"Courtesy of his bestest aunt in the whole wide world!" Frankie says, trying to imitate Chase to the best of her ability. "You know she also got him a push-pin map of the world for his birthday, right?"

"Oh, Jesus. Where in the world is Hadley Moreno. I swear if I step on pins like I did his Legos . . ."

"You'll scream in pain and then put them away like you always did." She snuggles further into me. "Do *you* think she'll be okay?"

"You're the expert on this; you would know better than I."

"I know what the books say, what my head says . . . but you've known her longer. It might be nice to get the inside information without having to think about it."

"Hadley's an actress. She's playing a part, but I hear her crying in the basement when she thinks she's alone. She's still hurting, and I think it'll be a long time before she can move on. The trial didn't help, but at least it's over."

"I wish she'd open up to someone. We could help her handle . . ."

"I love you, but there are some things you have to handle on your own. When your mom died, did you open up to anyone or turn inside?"

"I . . . point taken."

"I almost lost everything when I curled into my shell. You know all this; you were there. Sometimes, you have to be in the background, waiting to catch the person when they fall. We'll be there for her when she's ready to face it or move on. No matter what happens, we're her family, and that's never going to change."

"You ever think of expanding it?"

"What?"

"Our family." Frankie pulls out of my embrace and leans her head on my elbow. "I'm not saying right away, but is that something you might be open to?"

"Yeah, I'd very much be interested in that." The smile on my face spreads from ear to ear.

"I just . . . .there are so many that we could open our doors to. I think it would be good for Chase too. Especially with his roomie leaving for an undetermined amount of time."

"I agree wholeheartedly. There are so many options, and we don't have a ton of space, but we can add one more to our brood. Are you okay with that though? Is that what you really want? I know you always wanted to carry—"

"There might be options, but Chase already fell in love with one. The costs are a bit steep, but I think we can work it into our budget," Frankie says, continuing her conversation without hearing me.

"Costs? What?" I ask in confusion.

"At the shelter. Chase fell in love with this little nothing of a puppy named Hank. You should have seen him with Hank." She stops on a dime. "Wait, carry? Jasmine . . ." She lets my name hang out there in the ether.

"A dog? Dogs are good. Would teach Chase some responsibility, but he would have to take care of the pup. I don't want him making you walk the pupster because he's playing his games or something." I try to divert the conversation away from my words as the nerves build up in my chest.

"You want to have a child with me?" Frankie whispers.

"I always wanted a family with you. I thought you knew that."

"I do, but with our lives the way they are. . ."

"I want the world with you, whatever that entails. If you want a little Frankie running around driving her big brother crazy, I'm all for it."

"Or maybe we adopt and open our home to someone a little older? As I said, there are so many just hoping for a chance. Maybe we give it to them. Maybe we find that missing piece that turns my hair gray before I'm ready." Frankie laughs, pushing a strand of hair away from my face. "Who am I kidding? You'll go gray before I will."

"Probably, but I really like that idea."

"It's a much more arduous process."

"All the things worth having are. Until then, tell me about Hank."

"Hank, the nine-year-old 'wonder' puppy with three legs. Chase says he's a superhero like Hadley. He can still run, jump, and do everything little young ones do, but he's older. You should have seen them playing; the volunteer told me no one comes to see Hank at all. A senior dog with special needs rarely gets looked at."

"And you think he can handle it?"

"I think Chase is stronger than you and I combined. Besides, he insisted on leaving his name and his own money for the fees. I asked them to hold it to the side until I spoke with you, but I did fill out the paperwork."

"And when do we pick up Hank Steele?" I turn my attention back to Chase, whose laugh is the loudest of the gaggle of children.

"They'll come by tomorrow if I ask and do a quick inspection before dropping him off. If you're sure."

"We're getting a dog," I say with a soft laugh. Frankie snuggles back into me, and we try to enjoy our silence for a few more seconds.

"We're getting a dog," she concurs, snuggling in tight around my frame. Victor appears with Lillian by his side.

"You going to hide up here all day while we run the party or . . ." Victor says and smiles. The two finally found a place and roped us all into helping them move.

"Considering how many boxes of your clothing we had to move, you should be doing this free of charge," Frankie says before I can. She stands and pulls Lillian into a hug. Standing, I start to walk back to the chaotic children's party for my son.

"How's she doing?" Victor asks quietly.

"Surviving," I answer as we hear Hadley laugh as all the kids tackle her to the ground for the Frisbee.

***

The brisk wind off the water by Pier 6 reminds Hadley and me that the seasons are changing. A carry-on suitcase and backpack rest next to the railing. The helicopters are rising with their lights flashing off the farthest launch pad. Hadley's decision to walk away from all of us still stings. Surprisingly, it was Chase who reminded me that we did the same thing, just in our house. It's selfish of all of us to want her to stay, but watching her leave will be hard as hell.

"You have everything? I mean, that's a small amount considering what you left at my house," I say with a lightness in my tone.

"Yeah. I have my chargers, tablet, phone, and all the essentials." She reaches into her backpack and opens a box filled with small plastic jewelry bags. "The most important part of the trip." She takes out one bag, kneels as close to the pier's edge as possible, and empties the ash into the East River. "Today our journey begins."

Hadley stands up, her engagement ring hanging on a chain around her neck, and throws the empty bag into the garbage. Last month she got her first tattoo on the side of her foot: *Ma Puce,* or sweetie in French. Logan always ended their calls with that. The tattoo artist added some of his ashes into the black ink for everything to be as Hadley requested. Now she's going to see the world and leave a little bit of him behind every step of the way—together, as they planned for their honeymoon.

We all thought it was crazy, but Hadley said it best. "It's how I can heal. You don't have to understand, just respect my wishes." For the most part, we have. Victor and Will checked global laws while Frankie and I plotted some of the places she wanted to go. Chase taught her how to use her new cell phone for better pictures. And how to use her tablet's pencil for journal writing.

Once Chase opened up his birthday present, he went into overdrive. Hadley now has to send him a photo of every new place she goes. He gets to put it on the map, but also print the photo for a scrapbook. I'm thankful she went out of her way to do that; it will make her absence hurt less.

I watch as tears begin to roll down Hadley's face. Just because it is something she has to do, for work and herself, doesn't make it any easier. Not to mention she's planning a goodbye tour instead of a wedding.

"You know, death makes utterly no sense to me," she says, wiping away a residual tear hanging onto her lower eyelashes. "I understand the concept of it, the rationality of it, yet it still doesn't equate to anything. We humans are pulled toward it like cattle to the slaughter. Slow and steady through the barricades until we get a bolt to the head."

"Not to sound too Disney, but it's the circle of life. We can't live forever. We couldn't sustain it." I try to stick with factual information and not delve into the emotional.

"I don't want to die, Jazz." She shivers, and I'm not sure if it's the cold or fear.

"No one does." The words come out softly, but I know that's not what she wants to hear. "Death is the one thing I longed for more than anything else in the world during high school. Sometimes I still struggle with its pull of peace and serenity." I lean back from the railing, arms outstretched, trying to garner courage from the bitter breeze. "But it is also the most paralyzing fear that I have. The loss of Frankie, Chase, you, Victor, or the team . . . my home. It's overwhelming."

"How do you handle it?"

"I don't know if I'm the best person to ask about that. I mean, I still struggle, but therapy is helping."

"You faced it, and you still came back from it. How do you get through it when it overwhelms you?"

"Truthfully?" I say. She leans her back on the railing and looks at me, waiting. "When I think about death, it's a slow spiral. I might think of a memory with my oma. Then I remember she's gone and that turns into Mom dying. Then I think about my brother and how I'm next in line."

I take a deep breath and exhale slowly as I feel the same anxiety rising to take hold. "My mind keeps going along that path until I'm curled up in a ball on the floor of the shower or in my therapist's office. I find myself crying and begging for my thoughts to leave me alone. The fear of being forgotten, being cold underground, just not existing in any other plane—it makes me want to vomit. If an attack is really bad, I hit myself in the head too. As if a fist would calm the panic attack."

"You'll give yourself a concussion," she answers, trying to make me laugh a little. It works.

"Point is, they come and go. There's a moment when I can think of my family and what tomorrow will look like. I keep focusing on that, and eventually, it passes."

Hadley turns back around, her attention on the moonlight and Governor's Island in the distance. "I can't rationalize him in heaven or hell. It never made logical or scientific sense to him either. This was supposed to be our time to live and enjoy. And because of me . . ."

"Stop. Barrett's decisions are not on you. He's a sick man who interpreted things you did as an invitation. Social media and autographs do not give anyone the right to objectify, own, or control you, Hadley. I know it's hard, but you know it's true."

"I do, but if he never met me, Logan might still be alive."

"Ifs and maybes will prevent you from living."

"Maybe," she says with a half-smirk. "Logan would break everything down to the smallest little detail, enjoying a new level of depth like a kid with seven-layer cake. He showed me the world in a beautiful new way. How can I see it without him?"

"You don't." I wrap my arm around her to calm the shivers. "You view it with your eyes wide open. You experience it through the raw emotions and healing scars within you. Some colors may fade, never to be seen again, but some might brighten. In time that new light could reinvigorate everything you thought was lost."

"It's possible, but I can't stay here waiting for it to happen."

"I know."

Her head rests on my shoulder, her arms pulling me tightly into a hug. "Will you tell Chase every night that I love him to the moon and back? I'll text him as much as I can, but I want you to remind him."

"I promise."

"Make sure he keeps reading his comics and never allow him to grow up before he's ready. He's a good kid and he needs to enjoy his childhood as much as possible."

"Frankie and I will do our best. And stop talking like you're going away forever."

"It might be a long time," she says.

"Take all the time you need, Had."

"And make sure you take care of each other."

"We will," I say, starting to laugh. "Stop with the advice! You just worry about you."

"Love's hard to find, Jasmine, and you've been lucky to have a second chance. Don't fuck it up."

"Okay, Mom," I say with a huge grin. "You just keep in touch when you can, okay?"

"Of course."

Hadley pushes away from me, wiping her tears on my T-shirt. She shoves her hands in her pockets as we hear a helicopter getting closer.

"Where to first?"

"London premiere of the film, a ton of press junkets in Tokyo, Beijing, and then Sydney. I'm going to climb the bridge there and probably freak out my agent and management team."

The helicopter lands on the middle helipad. The blades continue to swirl as the door opens and someone gets out.

"Ms. Moreno, your luggage?" one of the crew asks. Hadley hands him the two bags.

"And after all that? You going to follow the plan or deviate?"

"I don't know. Maybe a little bit of both." She pulls out a note with the header *Hadley & Logan's Bucket List*. "Maybe it's time I start living life instead of just existing in it."

"And work?"

"I'll shoot things when they come up. That's the best part about my status now: people come to me, and I have contracts with guaranteed work."

"If anyone heard you now, they'd say you were a snob."

"I know, but I worked my ass off for that right." The pilot walks up and stands at attention.

"Ms. Moreno, we're ready for you. The gentleman over there will walk you to the chopper." He points to a man wearing a jumpsuit and helmet like he's in the military.

"I'll be right there." She turns to me and gives me another tight hug. "I'm going to miss you more than you know."

"Right back at you."

With one last squeeze, she's off with the crew members and hopping into the helicopter. I watch as the aircraft rises slowly from the ground before heading to its destination. It feels like the end of an era in my life, and the sadness that comes with it sucks. My phone vibrates with a message, and I pull it out to read.

I love you, sister from another mister.

Hadley's message warms my heart and pushes aside the fear of losing her. No matter what happens in the future, she's going to be in it. We've been a team since college. Life might change and adapt, but we're all in it together.

My phone buzzes again with a message from Karina; it's an address. I pull my keys out of my pocket, head to my car, and jump in and start driving.

Thirty minutes later, I'm pulling up to the side of the catholic school, and I see Will and Karina hugging the wall.

"What's going on?" I ask, heading to the entrance.

"Inside," Karina says before entering the building.

"Hadley get off okay?" Will asks.

"Yeah, she's good."

We walk into the gymnasium, and my throat clenches. A young woman lies on the floor, the school logo at half-court covered in blood. Her pants are wadded up and tossed to the side, her underwear torn, and a small knife lies next to her prone form. Will and Karina go to work walking the scene while I look at the poor girl on the floor.

No matter which way we turn or how we try to control it all, life and death always find a way. Whether we like it or not.

THE END

About Author

Kimberly Amato is the author of the Jasmine Steele Mystery Series and Enemy. Having won awards for a TV Pilot she co-wrote & produced, she dove headfirst into writing novels. Always creating, jotting down new ideas & unafraid to try new genres, Kimberly writes mysteries, crime, romance, sci-fi & more. Beyond that, she's a podcaster with her wife, Sheila, for the show Forever Fangirls reviewing TV and film on streaming services and in theaters. Kimberly enjoys keeping in touch with her readers. You can find her by using the links below or going to her website KimberlyAmato.com.

a

amazon.com/stores/Kimberly-Amato/author/B00RKJDIXA

BB

bookbub.com/authors/kimberly-amato

f

facebook.com/thekimberlyamato

O

instagram.com/kimberlyamato

Go to the link below to stay up to date on new releases and more!
https://www.kimberlyamato.com/newsletter

Also By Kimberly Amato

THE STEELE SERIES

Steele Intent (Book 1)

Melting Steele (Book 2)

Breaking Steele (Book 3)

Cold Steele (Book 4)

Steele Shield (Book 5)

Steele Influence (Book 6)

STANDALONES

Enemy

Milton Keynes UK
Ingram Content Group UK Ltd.
UKHW030629071024
449371UK00001B/231

9 780999 043387